A seventh-grade game . . .

Bruce stood up and walked toward Elizabeth. What's going on? Why is he coming over here? *She had a funny feeling she wasn't going to like whatever was going to happen next.*

Before she knew what was going on, Bruce was sitting down in front of her, craning his face toward hers. When she saw him pucker up his lips, she thought she was going to faint. I'm supposed to kiss him, *she realized in horror. She looked around at all the expectant faces, then back at Bruce.*

Just as Bruce was about to plant his lips on top of her own, she quickly turned her face so that the kiss landed on her cheek.

"Hey, what's the big idea?" Bruce asked in an exasperated tone. "Don't you know how to play this game?"

The whole room erupted in laughter. Elizabeth was paralyzed. She opened her mouth, but she couldn't say anything. Tears began to form in her eyes.

D1340233

Sweet Valley Twins titles, published by Bantam Books. Ask your bookseller for titles you have missed:

SWEET VALLEY TWINS

Elizabeth the Seventh-Grader

Written by
Jamie Suzanne

Created by
FRANCINE PASCAL

BANTAM BOOKS
TORONTO • NEW YORK • LONDON • SYDNEY • AUCKLAND

ELIZABETH THE SEVENTH-GRADER
A BANTAM BOOK 0 553 40834 8

Originally published in USA by Bantam Books

First publication in Great Britain

PRINTING HISTORY
Bantam edition published 1995

The trademarks "Sweet Valley" and "Sweet Valley Twins"
are owned by Francine Pascal and are used under licence by
Bantam Books and Transworld Publishers Ltd.

Conceived by Francine Pascal.

Produced by Daniel Weiss Associates, Inc,
33 West 17th Street, New York, NY 10011

Cover photo by Oliver Hunter

Bantam Books are published by Transworld Publishers Ltd,
61–63 Uxbridge Road, Ealing, London W5 5SA,
in Australia by Transworld Publishers (Australia) Pty Ltd,
15–25 Helles Avenue, Moorebank, NSW 2170,
and in New Zealand by Transworld Publishers (NZ) Ltd,
3 William Pickering Drive, Albany, Auckland.

Printed and bound in Great Britain by
Cox & Wyman Ltd, Reading, Berkshire

To Michael Ari Groopman

One

"Want to go to the mall after school tomorrow?" Jessica Wakefield asked her identical twin sister, Elizabeth. "I need to buy some things for the sixth-grade camping trip. It's less than two weeks away."

"Hmmm?" Elizabeth mumbled as she pushed her chicken potpie around her plate. It was Monday night, and the girls were eating dinner in the kitchen. Their older brother, Steven, was at his friend Joe Howell's house. Their parents were at a meeting with Elizabeth's teachers, and Elizabeth was a nervous wreck. Why had her teachers called a special conference with her parents?

"I *asked* if you wanted to go to the mall tomorrow," Jessica repeated impatiently.

"Uh, yeah, sure. That sounds like a good idea, I guess," Elizabeth said distractedly.

Jessica raised an eyebrow. "Excuse me, but what

planet are you on? You're nowhere near Earth, that's for sure."

Elizabeth let out a half-laugh. "I guess I'm just thinking about that teachers' conference. Don't you think Mom and Dad should be home by now? What could they be talking about for so long?"

"Maybe they're discussing your eating habits," Jessica said, looking thoughtful.

"My eating habits?" Elizabeth repeated. "What are you talking about?"

Jessica pointed to Elizabeth's milk. Elizabeth looked down and gasped. "What s this stuff floating in it?" she asked in shock.

Jessica burst out laughing. "That's what milk looks like when you pour pepper into it," she said through her giggles.

Elizabeth flushed and pushed her milk aside. "I guess I'm just a little distracted."

"Yeah, maybe I should take that pepper away from you before you do something dangerous to yourself," Jessica teased.

"Ha ha," Elizabeth said listlessly. "Seriously, Jess, I just wish I knew what that meeting's about. I don't think I've done anything wrong recently."

"You probably just failed a test or something," Jessica suggested.

Elizabeth frowned. "I *did* finish that math test really fast yesterday. Come to think of it, I was the first one in the whole class to hand it in. What if there was a whole section of questions I didn't even get to?"

"Come on, Lizzie, I was just joking," Jessica said. "You're incapable of failing a test—it's just not in you.

And when was the last time you got in trouble for *anything*?"

She's right, Elizabeth admitted to herself. Jessica was the twin who was always getting herself in trouble, not Elizabeth. The girls were identical on the outside, with their long blond hair, blue-green eyes, and dimple in their left cheek, but the similarities ended there.

Elizabeth was the more serious and studious of the twins. She worked hard in all her classes at Sweet Valley Middle School. In her free time, she enjoyed having long talks with her friends, reading a good mystery, or working on the sixth-grade newspaper, the *Sixers*. Not only had she helped start the paper, but she was also the editor-in-chief.

Jessica, on the other hand, spent most of her spare time with the Unicorn Club, a group of the prettiest and most popular girls in the school. She'd choose gossiping on the phone with one of her friends over doing her homework any day. Elizabeth thought Jessica's Unicorn friends were silly and referred to them as "the Snob Squad." All they seemed to care about were boys, parties, clothes, and rock stars. But despite their differences, Jessica and Elizabeth were as close as two sisters could be.

"I just wish I knew for sure that my teachers aren't saying anything horrible," Elizabeth said, crumpling her paper napkin into a ball.

"I think you're being paranoid, Elizabeth," Jessica said. "I mean, when Mr. Bowman phoned this afternoon, Mom didn't seem *that* upset."

Elizabeth's eyes widened. "What do you mean, *that* upset?"

"She was only crying for a few minutes," Jessica said breezily.

Elizabeth gasped. "She was *crying*?"

Jessica's lip began to quiver and she burst out laughing. "Really, Lizzie, I'm beginning to think that all that studying is having a bad effect on your brain. You'll believe *anything*."

"OK, OK," Elizabeth said, looking down at her plate to hide her embarrassment. "If you were around when Mr. Bowman called, tell me what really happened."

Jessica sighed heavily. "What really happened was Mom said, 'That was Mr. Bowman. Your dad and I have to go in for a conference with him and some of Elizabeth's other teachers this evening. There are two chicken potpies in the freezer. Just stick them in the microwave for ten minutes and let them cool off a little.'"

"That's it?"

"That's it," Jessica confirmed. Then she snapped her fingers and her face clouded over. "Except—there was *one* other thing."

"What?" Elizabeth asked, feeling her stomach turn over. "What was it?"

"She said there was lettuce in the fridge if we wanted a salad," Jessica said, unable to control her giggles.

It's nine thirty . . . where could they be? Elizabeth flopped over in her bed, imagining all the horrible things Mr. Bowman and her other teachers could be saying to her parents. *Mr. and Mrs. Wakefield, I'm sorry* to have to tell you that Elizabeth is being kicked out of school. All along, we've led you to believe she was a good student, but lately, her work just hasn't been up to her normal standards. Then her mother would burst into tears, and her father would take his wife's hand for support.

Elizabeth knew her fears were silly, but she couldn't help feeling this way. Her parents had never been called in for a special conference about her.

But if I did something wrong, I'd know about it, wouldn't I? Elizabeth reasoned. *Maybe Jessica did something wrong, and Mr. Bowman thought it was me.* It wouldn't be the first time Elizabeth got in trouble for something her twin did.

When she heard a knock at her door, she practically rolled off her bed. "Come in," she called weakly.

Slowly the door opened, and her parents appeared in the doorway.

"Good. You're still awake," said Mrs. Wakefield, a serious expression on her face.

That's it. I've done something awful, Elizabeth thought as her parents walked stiffly into her room.

"Elizabeth, honey, we need to talk to you about something very serious," Mr. Wakefield said.

Elizabeth sat straight up in bed. "Is it the math test yesterday? Or have I been whispering with Amy too much in class?"

Amy Sutton was Elizabeth's best friend after Jessica. Amy worked on the *Sixers* with Elizabeth and was also a serious student. The two of them weren't exactly troublemakers, but they did whisper in class sometimes.

"You didn't do anything wrong," Mrs. Wakefield said, pushing a strand of Elizabeth's long blond hair behind her ear.

"I didn't?" Elizabeth asked timidly.

"As a matter of fact, you've been doing everything too well," Mr. Wakefield said, smiling at Mrs. Wakefield and winking.

Elizabeth frowned. "I don't get it."

"Mr. Bowman and your other teachers think you've been doing so well in all your classes that you belong on a higher level," Mrs. Wakefield explained. "They think you're not being challenged enough in the sixth grade."

"I'm still not following you," Elizabeth said. "What do they mean *on a higher level*?"

"Do you want to tell her or should I?" Mrs. Wakefield asked Mr. Wakefield.

"Come on, somebody tell me what's going on," Elizabeth urged. "The suspense is killing me."

Mr. Wakefield swallowed hard. "Your teachers think you should be in the seventh grade," he blurted out, beaming proudly at his daughter.

Seventh grade! Elizabeth couldn't believe what she was hearing. "Are you joking?"

"We're completely serious," Mrs. Wakefield said. "We're so proud of you, Elizabeth. You've really been working hard lately, and it's certainly paid off. Mr. Bowman said you're the star of your grade."

Elizabeth was stunned. "I—I don't know what to say. I mean, I thought I was in some kind of trouble. I never in a million years thought that *this* would happen."

Mrs. Wakefield smiled. "It's natural to be confused, honey. And just because your teachers suggested you skip a grade doesn't mean you have to. If you'd rather stay in sixth grade, that's fine."

"Stay in sixth grade?" Elizabeth repeated, looking from one parent to the other. Then she smiled broadly and threw her arms around both her parents. "Are you kidding? This is the most exciting thing that ever happened to me! I can't wait to try harder courses and get to know older kids and—"

"Slow down, honey," Mrs. Wakefield said, laughing. "You don't have to make up your mind right away. This is a really big decision, and you should think about it carefully."

"Your mother's right," Mr. Wakefield said. "You have to consider what being a seventh-grader will mean. You won't be spending as much time with your friends, and you won't be spending as much time with Jessica."

Elizabeth leaned back and thought. *It's fun to be in the same classes with Jessica, but we could still hang out a lot,* she reasoned. *I mean, it's not like we can really talk during classes anyway, and we do live in the same house.* And Elizabeth figured that she could see her friends at lunch, and they could get together outside of school as often as they did before.

"I don't think that's a problem at all," Elizabeth said after a few minutes of reflection.

"You also need to think about the different social scene," Mr. Wakefield continued. "Things are bound to be a little . . . faster in seventh grade."

"How different could it be?" Elizabeth asked. She

thought the idea of hanging out with seventh-graders was totally great. They would be more mature than sixth-graders, and even though she loved her friends, she was sure that socializing with older kids would be challenging and exciting. Normally, Jessica was the one who always wanted to be older than she was and who complained about how babyish the sixth-graders were. But if Elizabeth was ahead of her grade academically, wouldn't she fit in well with older kids?

"All your father and I want you to do is think long and hard about this before you tell your teachers what you want to do," Mrs. Wakefield said.

Elizabeth grinned. "OK, OK, I'll think about it tonight and tomorrow morning, and I'll let you know what I've decided tomorrow after school."

"Atta girl," Mr. Wakefield said, kissing her on the forehead.

"Sleep well," Mrs. Wakefield added, tucking her in.

I'm going to be in the seventh grade! Elizabeth thought as her parents turned off her light and left her room. *I'm the happiest girl in Sweet Valley!*

Two

"I have something really incredible to tell you," Elizabeth said to Jessica on Tuesday morning as the twins crossed the Wakefields' front lawn on their way to school. Elizabeth felt as if she would burst if she didn't tell her sister her news about skipping to seventh grade.

"Well, I have something really incredible to tell *you*," Jessica said, kicking a rock into the gutter. "Something Lila told me on the phone last night that totally bummed me out."

Elizabeth sighed. Lila Fowler was Jessica's best friend after Elizabeth and the wealthiest girl in Sweet Valley Middle School. Elizabeth thought Lila was incredibly snobby and couldn't imagine that she'd told Jessica anything very important. Still, Elizabeth knew that Jessica wouldn't listen to her big news if something else was on her mind. "What did she say?" Elizabeth asked.

"Tom McKay's having this great party on Friday," Jessica said, frowning. "It sounds like it's going to be *the* party of the year."

"So what's wrong with that?" Elizabeth asked, laughing. "You love parties."

"Yeah, but I'm not invited," Jessica said gloomily.

"*You?* You're always invited to parties and stuff," Elizabeth said, turning to look directly at her sister. "Why wouldn't you be invited?"

"Because it's just for seventh- and eighth-graders," Jessica moaned. "Janet tried to get Tom to make an exception for the Unicorns, but he said if he let one sixth-grader go, he'd have to let all of us go."

Janet Howell was an eighth-grader and the president of the Unicorn Club. She also happened to be Lila's first cousin and the most popular girl in the entire school.

"Just for seventh- and eighth-graders, huh?" Elizabeth mused, feeling an unexpected flicker of excitement. She normally didn't care about parties all that much, but she liked the idea of being included among the older kids.

"Can you believe it?" Jessica said in an outraged voice. "I, Jessica Wakefield, can't go to the coolest party of the year just because I have the bad luck to be a sixth-grader."

Elizabeth bit her lip. Jessica looked really hurt and disappointed. There was no way she could tell her sister her news now. "I bet the party will be pretty boring anyway," Elizabeth said comfortingly. "I mean, how fun could it be if no sixth-graders are there?"

"Are you crazy? It'll be a blast," Jessica said mournfully. "All the coolest people in the school are going to be at Tom's party—except me, of course." She groaned dramatically. "I *hate* being in sixth grade. It's so boring. Seventh-graders get to have all the fun."

"Mmm," Elizabeth mumbled, feeling a secret thrill as she and Jessica turned to walk up the front lawn of the school. "I wonder if you're right."

"Steven, stop eating your salad with your fingers," Jessica snapped as the Wakefields dug into their dinner on Tuesday night. "We're in a nice restaurant, not a zoo."

"Oh, really? I thought we *were* at a zoo," Steven said, picking up another piece of lettuce with his hand. "You look a lot like a monkey with your hair like that."

"Shut up, Steven," Jessica muttered, running her fingers along the smooth French braid going down her back. "You just can't appreciate a nice hairstyle because you don't have any taste."

The Wakefields were eating dinner at La Maison Jacques, the best restaurant in Sweet Valley. Jessica had no idea why her parents had taken them there. It wasn't anyone's birthday or anything.

"Speaking of taste," Steven teased, "that dress you're wearing looks almost exactly like the living room curtains. Except not as nice." He guffawed at his own stupid joke.

"I'll ignore your immature comment," Jessica said, cutting her salmon with her fork and knife.

"I'm trying to concentrate on my delicious meal."

"Oh, right. I forgot you can't eat and talk at the same time," Steven said, slapping his palm on his forehead. "I know it's hard for you to do too many things at once."

"Mom and Dad, can we leave Steven at home the next time we go out for a nice dinner?" Jessica asked, putting her fork down on her plate. "It's difficult to enjoy a good meal with such a child around."

"Could you two please stop your bickering?" Mr. Wakefield said impatiently. "Elizabeth has an important announcement to make."

Jessica turned to look at Elizabeth, who was eating her coq au vin in almost complete silence. *Maybe she really is in trouble*, Jessica thought, remembering how worried her sister had been about the conference with her teachers. Elizabeth had wanted to tell her something on their way to school that morning, but Jessica never found out what it was. And before they'd left the house, Elizabeth had gone into her father's study with both her parents and shut the door. Jessica hadn't thought much of it, but now she was starting to wonder. *Maybe for the first time in her life Elizabeth actually messed up.*

Elizabeth was still staring at her dinner, not saying a word.

"What's going on, Lizzie?" Jessica asked finally.

Elizabeth took a deep breath and looked at her parents, who were gazing at her expectantly.

"Well," Elizabeth began slowly. "Um . . . remember how Mom and Dad had that meeting with my teachers last night at school?"

"Don't tell me. You got a *B* on a paper," Steven said, grabbing a roll from the bread basket.

"This is serious, Steven," Mr. Wakefield said sternly. "Listen to what your sister's about to say."

Elizabeth squirmed in her seat. "Well, they think . . . I mean, my teachers think, that I should just, uh . . . well, just skip the rest of sixth grade and, um . . . start seventh grade. Right away."

Jessica almost spat out her sip of water. She pushed her chair back from the table with a loud screech. "*What?*" she demanded, her face getting hot.

Mrs. Wakefield smiled brightly. "Elizabeth is going to be in the seventh grade," she repeated. "Isn't that fabulous news?"

"I think we should all raise our glasses," Mr. Wakefield said as he clinked his wineglass with Mrs. Wakefield's.

Jessica's heart pounded in her chest. "E-Elizabeth can't be in seventh grade," she sputtered. "I'm the one with friends in seventh grade. If anyone belongs in the seventh grade, it's me, not Elizabeth!"

Mr. Wakefield gazed at her for a moment before he spoke. "This isn't about having friends in the seventh grade," he said calmly. "Elizabeth is skipping to seventh grade because she's been doing so well in school all year. You should be happy for your sister—this is a great honor for her."

"But y-you can't be in the seventh grade," Jessica said, looking into her sister's eyes. "We won't be in the same classes anymore. We'll never see each other."

"Of course we'll see each other," Elizabeth said firmly. "Just not in class."

"But it won't be the same," Jessica said, her eyes filling with tears. "We won't be studying for the same tests and everything together."

"Jess, it's not like we study together now," Elizabeth pointed out.

"Yeah, I didn't think you ever studied, Jessica," Steven teased.

"Be quiet, Steven. Nobody's talking to you," Jessica barked. She wiped her eyes and sat up straight. "No offense, Lizzie, but of the two of us, I'm the one who's a little more mature—socially, I mean."

"Obviously, you're not as sophisticated as you think," Steven said. "You're not the one who's skipping sixth grade."

"Steven, cut it out," Jessica said.

"Jessica, I think *you* should cut it out, too," Mr. Wakefield said. "We're here to celebrate this exciting thing that's happening to your sister, and you're just being negative."

"It's OK," Elizabeth said softly. "Jessica's just upset, and I think I understand why." She turned to Jessica and smiled. "It'll take some getting used to, but you'll see that things will be just the way they've always been. We'll be as close as ever."

Jessica put her fork down. She wasn't in the mood for salmon anymore. She wasn't even in the mood for dessert. *Nothing's going to be the same*, she thought miserably. *Elizabeth and I belong together. Now she'll get to do all the fun things without me.*

*   *   *

"Hey, Mom said to tell you to hurry up," Steven said on Wednesday morning, poking his head into Jessica's room from the hallway. "Dad made French toast for breakfast, and it smells pretty awesome."

Jessica was sitting slouched on her bed, fiddling with the lacy edge of her pillow sham. "French toast is the last thing I care about right now," she mumbled. "In fact, I don't feel much like going to school today."

"What's your problem?" Steven asked as he walked all the way into the room. "Are you having a bad hair day or something?"

"Go down and inhale your French toast, Steven. I'm really not in the mood," Jessica said.

"Let me guess," Steven said. "You're sill irked about Elizabeth being in seventh grade."

Just hearing those words gave Jessica a headache. "It's not fair," she groaned. "We're supposed to be in the same grade. That's one of the rules of being twins."

Steven leaned casually against the doorway. "You know, to tell you the truth, I'm not really crazy about Elizabeth being in seventh grade either. Those older kids can be pretty . . . wild. I don't think she's ready for it."

"Well, no one else seems to realize that," Jessica grumbled.

"That's why you're lucky that Super Steven is here to help you out."

Jessica arched her eyebrow. "*Super* Steven? What's *that* supposed to mean?"

"It just so happens that you're talking to an expert on psychology," Steven boasted. "I'm a student of human behavior."

"Oh, please, give me a break," Jessica said, rolling her eyes.

"I'm serious," Steven went on. "All you need to use on Elizabeth is a little reverse psychology."

Jessica sat up. "Huh?"

"Oh, sorry," Steven said. "I forgot you don't understand such big words."

Jesscia tossed her pillow at him. "Steven, if you don't have anything to say, just get out," she ordered, glaring at him.

"Geez, so jumpy," Steven said, catching the pillow.

"Steven!"

"OK, OK. All I'm saying is, if you start making Elizabeth think that her being in the seventh grade is the greatest thing in the world, she might change her mind about it," Steven explained.

Jessica frowned. "And how, Mr. Expert on Psychology, will that make Elizabeth change her mind?"

"If you act like you're really happy about her being in seventh grade, she'll think you won't care about not being with her," Steven explained.

"Hmm," Jessica mumbled, frowning in concentration. "You know, it's hard to believe, but I think you might actually have a good idea."

"That's me, the expert on—"

"I could act like being in seventh grade isn't so great after all," Jessica broke in, her eyes lighting up.

"And I could pretend like sixth grade is a total blast, so she'll really miss it."

"Now you're getting it," Steven said.

Jessica giggled. "I could even start moving in on her territory, so she'll be *really* jealous. Like I could start hanging out with her boring friends and working on that dumb newspaper and stuff," she said excitedly.

"Exactly," Steven said, as if Jessica had figured out a complicated math problem that only he knew the answer to. "She'll be the one who's jealous of you, instead of the other way around. You'll seem so happy without her that her feelings will be hurt, and she'll come running back to the sixth grade as fast as you can say French toast."

"French toast!" Jessica exclaimed as she jumped off her bed. "Come on. I'm starving."

"I'll race you downstairs," Steven said.

Jessica turned to face him. "You know, for an annoying older brother, you're pretty smart sometimes."

"I wish I had a tape recorder with me," Steven said as he headed for the door.

"Hi, Amy!" Elizabeth said as she walked up to Amy's locker on Wednesday morning.

"Hi, Elizabeth," Amy said, closing her locker door. "You're just the person I wanted to see. I thought we could go over the article I'm working on about the camping trip before homeroom."

"Forget about the article," Elizabeth said dismissively. "I've got some amazing news."

Amy raised her eyebrows. "What's up? Did you come up with a new idea for the paper or something?"

"No, it's nothing like that." Elizabeth took a deep breath and shuffled her feet nervously. "What I wanted to tell you is . . . my teachers have decided that I should skip the rest of sixth grade and go right to seventh!"

Amy's eyes widened in shock. For a moment, she just stared at Elizabeth, not saying a word. Then her face broke into a grin. "You're right—that *is* amazing news. The most amazing news I've heard all week, in fact." She shook her head. "Make that all month. All year, even. You must be totally excited."

"Excited isn't the word for it," Elizabeth said, beaming. "I'm absolutely ecstatic. I feel like I'm jumping out of my skin."

"Then I'm happy for you," Amy said, smiling back. "Your parents must be so proud."

Elizabeth blushed. "Yeah, they really are. I think they're as excited as I am."

Amy leaned against her locker and peered thoughtfully into space. "I guess your life will be really different now."

"I doubt it will be *that* different," Elizabeth said as the homeroom bell rang overhead.

"Well, we better go to homeroom," Amy said, then frowned. "Or are you even in my homeroom anymore?"

"I guess this is my last day," Elizabeth answered. "I'm supposed to start my new schedule tomorrow."

Amy shook her head in amazement. "I can't believe it, Elizabeth. This is all happening so fast!"

"I know!" Elizabeth exclaimed as she floated down the hall with her friend. "It's so wonderful, I almost feel like I'm dreaming!"

Three

"Hey, Elizabeth, I hear you're skipping ahead to high school," Caroline Pearce said as she walked by Elizabeth's lunch table on Wednesday. Elizabeth was sitting with her friends Maria Slater, Amy, Winston Egbert, and Todd Wilkins, her sort-of boyfriend. "You're *so* lucky—you'll get to hang out with all the high school guys and stuff."

Elizabeth glanced at Amy. Caroline was the biggest gossip in the school, and she usually got her information twisted around. "Actually, Caroline, I'm not going to Sweet Valley High."

"You're not?" Caroline asked, frowning. "Well, *I* heard that you are—and that you'll be on the high school cheerleading squad, too."

Elizabeth choked back her laughter. "Well, I *am* skipping sixth grade, but I'm just going to seventh, not high school." She exchanged another glance with Amy. "And as far as I know, I'm not going to be a cheerleader."

Caroline looked a little disappointed. "Oh, well, I guess that's still pretty cool," she said finally. "Congratulations anyway."

"Thanks," Elizabeth said as Caroline walked to another table.

"So how does it feel to be on your way to Sweet Valley High?" Todd asked Elizabeth.

Elizabeth giggled. "To tell you the truth, it's pretty weird to think this is my last day as a sixth-grader."

"Yeah, I guess from now on, you'll be eating lunch with seventh-graders," Amy added.

"I don't see why I would stop sitting with you guys," Elizabeth said. "I mean, you'll still be my best friends. We just won't have classes together, that's all."

"Don't you think you'll want to hang out with your new classmates?" Amy asked.

"Yeah, you'll probably have lots more to talk about with the seventh-graders than you do with us, since you'll have the same teachers and all," Maria agreed.

"I hope you don't get swept away by some seventh-grade guy," Todd teased.

"Not a chance," Elizabeth assured him. "And there's no way I'll find the seventh-graders the tiniest bit more interesting than you guys."

As Elizabeth looked up, she saw Rick Hunter, a seventh-grader and one of the cutest guys in the school, walking right toward her.

"So, Wakefield, I hear you're a genius," Rick said, stopping at the table. "An IQ of 200—that's pretty impressive."

Elizabeth raised her eyebrows in surprise.

"Actually, I don't know what my IQ is, but I seriously doubt I qualify as a genius."

Rick frowned. "What's the deal with all the rumors, then?"

"Elizabeth's leaving us little sixth-graders and joining you and your seventh-graders," Amy explained.

Rick grinned. "You're skipping a grade?"

Elizabeth nodded, blushing.

"That's awesome, Wakefield. Maybe you'll be in some of my classes," Rick said, starting to walk away. "Catch you later."

"Yeah. 'Bye," Elizabeth called after him.

Todd watched Rick walk away. "You should really watch out for those guys," he warned Elizabeth.

"What guys?" Elizabeth asked.

"The seventh-grade guys, like Rick," Todd replied, shaking his head. "Seventh-grade guys aren't like sixth-grade guys. They think they're really cool, and they'll do anything to impress you."

Elizabeth laughed. "But you're friends with seventh-graders."

"That's different," Todd said, squirming in his seat.

"Oh, really? How's that?" Elizabeth asked playfully.

"I'm a guy," Todd said. "Older guys treat younger girls differently from the way they treat younger guys."

"Well, I'm sure I can take care of myself," Elizabeth said, smiling.

*   *   *

Come on, hurry up, Elizabeth thought impatiently as she sat in her last sixth-grade class, staring at the clock. The minute hand seemed to be permanently glued to five minutes before three. After school Mrs. Arnette, her social studies teacher, was going to give her her new schedule, and Elizabeth couldn't wait.

A million different thoughts raced through her head. *I wonder what books I'll be reading,* she mused. *I bet they'll be way more grown up and interesting than my sixth-grade books.*

Finally, the bell rang, and Elizabeth felt as though her whole body was trembling with nervousness and excitement.

"Hey, Elizabeth, do you want to go over to the *Sixers* office with me?" Amy asked as she gathered up her books from the desk right next to Elizabeth's. "I wanted to go over my article with you before the staff meeting."

"I'll have to meet you there," Elizabeth said. "Mrs. Arnette's supposed to tell me my new schedule now."

"Oh, right," Amy said, snapping her fingers. "I forgot."

"I'll be there in time for the meeting," Elizabeth said. "This shouldn't take long."

Elizabeth practically knocked over her chair as she walked to Mrs. Arnette's desk at the front of the room. *Stay calm,* she told herself. *Seventh-graders shouldn't act too silly and spastic.*

"Why don't you pull a chair up to my desk?" Mrs. Arnette said as Elizabeth came closer.

Elizabeth tried to catch her breath as she pulled a

chair up from the front row and sat down next to Mrs. Arnette.

"Your new teachers have compiled a list of your new classes," Mrs. Arnette said as she pulled down the black hairnet that covered her gray bun. Most of her students called her "the Hairnet," because she wore a hairnet to school every day.

Elizabeth looked down at the computer printout on the desk. She felt like jumping from excitement when she saw the words "Elizabeth Wakefield's Schedule" written at the top.

It's so incredible, Elizabeth thought, holding the schedule in her hands as if it were a delicate piece of lace or glass. She scanned down the page and looked at the names of her different classes. They all sounded so challenging—she couldn't believe she'd be taking intermediate French and pre-algebra.

"I also have all the books you're going to need for your new classes," Mrs. Arnette went on as she reached under her desk and pulled up a stack of books. "And here are the assignments you're going to have to catch up on."

Mrs. Arnette handed Elizabeth a huge pile of papers, and as Elizabeth flipped through them, she felt a quick stab of panic. She'd never had to do so much work before—she'd have to write about ten papers for her English class that semester and take about twenty quizzes and exams for pre-algebra. *Can I really do all this work?* she wondered.

"Now, Elizabeth, as you can see, there's a lot that's going to be expected of you, and it might seem overwhelming," Mrs. Arnette cautioned. "There's still time to change your mind." She looked right into Elizabeth's eyes. "You don't *have* to do this. It's purely your decision."

Elizabeth looked down at the stack of papers and books in front of her and back at Mrs. Arnette. Then she took a deep breath. "I'm not turning back now," she announced triumphantly as she stood up and hugged the stack of books to her chest. "I'm ready to hit these books and join seventh grade!"

Elizabeth whistled all the way to the *Sixers* office with her new books and assignment sheets in her backpack. *It's official*, she thought. *I'm really a seventh-grader.*

She flung open the *Sixers* office door. "Hi, everybody. Sorry I'm—" She broke off and gasped. Not only had they started the staff meeting without her, but Amy was sitting in her chair! Nobody ever sat in that chair besides Elizabeth. It was the editor-in-chief's chair, and everyone knew that.

"Um—what's going on?" Elizabeth asked carefully, trying to keep her voice under control.

Amy looked at Julie Porter, then at Elizabeth. "Mr. Bowman stopped by a little while ago and explained some changes at the paper."

"Like what kind of changes?" Elizabeth asked, feeling her cheeks get warm.

"Well, he said that since you're in the seventh grade now, you'll probably be working on the *Sweet Valley 7&8 Gazette* instead of the *Sixers*," Amy said slowly. "So he made me the new acting editor-in-chief."

Elizabeth looked around the room and realized that everyone was looking right at her, waiting for a response. She felt so stunned that she didn't know what to say. It had never occurred to her that she wouldn't be working for the *Sixers* anymore.

"Congratulations, Amy," Elizabeth said. "You'll make a great editor-in-chief."

"Thanks," Amy said, smiling weakly. "I'm sure it won't be the same without you. We'll try to follow your example."

"I'm sure it will be better than ever," Elizabeth said, smiling as cheerfully as she could. The truth was that she felt incredibly strange. Being on the *Sixers* was one of the things she loved the most. And since she'd helped found the paper, she felt especially attached to it.

She took a deep breath. *Get a grip*, she told herself. *You're a seventh-grader now, and working on the 7&8 Gazette will be pretty great—probably even better than working on the* Sixers.

"We'll all really miss you," Julie said sweetly.

"I'll miss you guys, too," Elizabeth said, smiling more easily now. She looked around the table and saw somebody she hadn't noticed before—Jessica!

"Too bad you have to quit the *Sixers* just when I've decided to join the staff," Jessica said gleefully.

Elizabeth raised her eyebrows. "You've *joined* the *Sixers*?"

"Yeah, well, I've always wanted to try my hand at journalism, so I thought now would be as good a time as any," Jessica explained.

Elizabeth looked at her sister skeptically. *This is the*

first time I've heard about her wanting to be a journalist.

"Aren't you excited I'm finally giving journalism a try?" Jessica asked. "I mean, I know how much you loved working on the *Sixers* and everything. I figured journalism talent must be in the blood."

"Uh, yeah. Right," Elizabeth said, staring at her sister, who was now happily scribbling something in her notebook.

"Anyway . . ." Amy said, her voice trailing off as she started rustling through some of her papers.

"Well, I guess I'll be going, then," Elizabeth said, without moving.

"OK, see you later," Amy said.

"Right," Elizabeth said. "'Bye, everybody."

"Good-bye, Elizabeth," Amy said, giving her a warm smile.

Elizabeth walked out of the office, a weird jealous feeling in her stomach. *It's OK,* she told herself. *What do I care whether Jessica works on the* Sixers *or not? I'm beyond the sixth-grade paper anyway. I'm on to bigger and better things—like the 7&8 Gazette!*

Four

◇

"There you are," Mrs. Wakefield said to Elizabeth on Wednesday afternoon. Elizabeth was walking up the front sidewalk after school just as her mother was unloading groceries from the car. "Did you find out about your new schedule?"

When Elizabeth saw her mother's proud smile, a thrill ran up her spine. She loved making her mother so happy.

"Mrs. Arnette gave me my new books and assignments," Elizabeth said as she picked up a grocery bag from the backseat of the car. "I start my new classes tomorrow. I'll have to do some reading and stuff tonight to catch up on everything I've missed this semester. The work looks really tough—but also really fun."

"I'm sure you'll do beautifully," Mrs. Wakefield said, beaming, as she and Elizabeth walked into the kitchen with the grocery bags. "I just want you to know how truly proud your father and I are of you—you've worked so hard, and it's very brave of you to give seventh grade a try."

"Thanks," Elizabeth said, blushing at her mother's praise.

"Of course, it's going to be difficult at first," Mrs. Wakefield continued. "You might get discouraged by all the work you're going to have to do."

For a moment, Elizabeth thought of all the assignments she'd have to catch up on. Some of them looked as if they'd be hard—but Elizabeth never backed away from a challenge, and that was one of the things that made her parents proud of her. "I'm sure I can handle it," she said confidently. "I won't let you down."

Primrose Place is starting in a few minutes," Jessica told Elizabeth on Wednesday night from the doorway of Elizabeth's bedroom. "Aren't you coming downstairs?"

Elizabeth looked up from her pre-algebra book and rubbed her eyes. *Primrose Place* was one of her and Jessica's favorite TV shows, and they tried not to miss any episodes.

"Actually, can you just let me know what happens later? I have too much work to do," Elizabeth said.

"Whatever," Jessica said lightly. "Do you want me to tape it for you?"

"That's OK," Elizabeth said, looking back at her book. "I don't think I'll have time to watch much television."

"I think it's really great that you're jumping right

in, getting started on all those tough assignments and everything," Jessica said as she twisted her hair up into a bun.

"Yeah, I can tell it'll be a lot of work, but so far it's been a fun challenge," Elizabeth admitted. Then she looked at her sister. "What do you mean *you* think it's great. I thought you said my skipping to seventh grade was a terrible idea."

"Oh, that," Jessica said breezily. "I changed my mind."

Elizabeth raised her eyebrows. "You did?"

"Mmm-hmm. I've been thinking about it, and I decided it's probably better for identical twins like us to have more distance from each other," Jessica said nonchalantly.

Distance from each other? Elizabeth repeated to herself. *I thought Jessica loved being together all the time—just like I did.*

"We're not going to have *that* much distance," Elizabeth pointed out.

"Well, now that I've started working at the *Sixers*, I'm not going to have that much extra time anymore," Jessica said. "Booster practice and Unicorn meetings take up enough of my spare time as it is. And I'm sure you'll be extra busy with all your schoolwork."

The Boosters were the cheering and baton-twirling squad for Sweet Valley Middle School.

"I could help you with your articles for the *Sixers* if you want," Elizabeth offered. "That way we could spend a little extra time together."

"Thanks, but Amy has already volunteered to help

me out. And Todd's going to be doing some guest editing on this issue, since there'll be a bunch of sports articles. He said he'd give me a hand, because he's already had some writing experience," Jessica said. "Todd and Amy are both really great, by the way."

Elizabeth raised her eyebrows. "I always thought you said they were both boring," she reminded her.

Jessica shrugged. "Well, I never really spent that much time with them before. I'll be getting to know both of them a lot better now." Jessica looked at her watch. "Oops! Time for the show," she announced cheerfully, sailing back through the door. "Are you sure you can't join me?"

Elizabeth looked at the stack of books sitting in front of her on her desk. *I'm just on math,* she thought. *I haven't even started English, history, and science yet.*

"I'm sure," she said. "You go ahead. It looks like I have a long night in front of me."

"No offense, but you look terrible," Jessica said to Elizabeth on Thursday morning as they walked up the front steps to school.

"Thanks for the compliment," Elizabeth said, then covered her mouth as she let out an enormous yawn. "When I woke up this morning, my head was on top of my history book. I think I slept about three hours all night."

"What a drag," Jessica said. "It's like you have so much work, you don't have a life anymore."

"I'm sure things will settle down when I get caught up," Elizabeth said dismissively.

"Hey, Amy! Hi, Maria!" Jessica called enthusiastically as she bounded toward where they were standing at the top of the steps.

"Hey, guys," Maria and Amy said at the same time.

"Amy, do you think we could get together after school and talk about my article?" Jessica asked as she put on some lip gloss.

"Sure, that would be great," Amy agreed.

"I can't wait to start writing," Jessica continued. "I think it'll get me even more psyched for the camping trip the weekend after next. Aren't you guys getting excited?"

"Yeah, it's going to be a blast," Maria agreed.

"I think it's going to be the social event of the year," Jessica said. She turned toward Elizabeth. "Sorry you're going to miss it, Lizzie."

Elizabeth smiled and shrugged. "Yeah, me too. But I guess I'll have a lot to keep me busy," she said, adjusting her full backpack on her shoulders.

"Speaking of busy," Jessica went on, turning back to Amy and Maria, "there's *so* much I have to do to get ready for the trip. I was thinking of going to the mall this weekend for a new sleeping bag. Do you guys want to come?"

"Sure," Amy said. "I need to get some stuff too."

"Cool!" Jessica said, peering at Elizabeth out of the corner of her eye.

I can't believe I'm really in my first seventh-grade class, Elizabeth thought as she walked into science class on Thursday morning. She took a deep breath and looked around the noisy room. There was a human skeleton hanging by the teacher's desk and posters of different kinds of apes and monkeys on the walls. *This looks so—advanced,* she thought.

Her heart pounding, she approached the teacher's desk.

"Excuse me," Elizabeth said softly to the teacher, Ms. Sawyer. "I'm Elizabeth Wakefield."

"Of course you are," Ms. Sawyer said, smiling sweetly underneath the heavy black-framed glasses, which seemed to cover most of her face. "Welcome to class."

"Thank you, Ms. Sawyer," Elizabeth said, shuffling her feet back and forth. "It's really great to be here."

Ms. Sawyer smiled, then looked back down at her notebook.

Isn't she going to tell me where to sit? Elizabeth wondered. *Or does she just expect me to stand here?*

After a few moments, Ms. Sawyer looked back up at her again. "Can I help you with something?"

"Uh . . . well . . . I was just wondering where I should sit," Elizabeth said.

Ms. Sawyer smiled warmly. "Anywhere you like. There's no assigned seating in seventh grade," she explained.

"Oh, right. Thanks," Elizabeth said, hoping that nobody noticed her question.

As she walked to an empty desk, the room grew completely quiet. The only sound she heard was her own footsteps. Elizabeth felt as if she were an animal in the zoo, being checked out by all the other students.

After what seemed like the longest walk of her life,

she found an empty seat in the back of the room. She took out her spiral notebook and science textbook.

"You have to put that away," the girl who was sitting next to her advised.

"How come?" Elizabeth asked.

"We're about to have a quiz," the girl informed her.

"We are?" Elizabeth asked incredulously.

"Yeah, we have one every Thursday," she answered. "It's a drag."

Wow, a quiz on my first morning as a seventh-grader, Elizabeth thought. She couldn't tell if the feeling in her stomach was from nerves or excitement. She hadn't really prepared for a quiz. *Please let it be about the stuff I read last night,* she thought as Ms. Sawyer handed her the single sheet of paper.

There were ten multiple-choice questions about different kinds of human bones. Luckily, Elizabeth had read that section of the book pretty thoroughly. She started marking off the answers, and before she knew it, it was over.

That wasn't so bad, she thought as she handed her finished quiz to the girl who was in charge of collecting them. *In fact, I think I did pretty well.*

Ms. Sawyer instructed the class to start reading the next assigned chapter while she sat at her desk correcting the quizzes.

When the teacher started handing back the quizzes, the room was full of whispers.

"That Wakefield girl got an *A*-plus," someone near the front of the room said.

"Yeah, I hear she's a genius," another person added.

Elizabeth was confused and excited and anxious all at once. *How could they know what I got on the quiz?* she wondered. *But what if they're right? What if I actually got an A-plus on my first seventh-grade quiz?*

"Nice job," Ms. Sawyer said as she put the quiz on Elizabeth's desk. "You're off to a great start."

Feeling pleased, Elizabeth looked down at the sheet of paper. A big *B*-plus was staring back at her. She knew it was a good grade, but she couldn't help feeling disappointed. *I'll just have to work harder than ever!* she decided.

"So how's your first morning as a seventh-grader going?" Amy asked Elizabeth as they stood in the lunch line in the cafeteria.

"It's OK," Elizabeth said, grabbing a turkey sandwich from the counter. "I didn't do as well as I would've liked on a science quiz this morning, though."

"Well, it *is* only your first day," Amy pointed out. "Give yourself a break."

"I guess you're right," Elizabeth said. "I just wanted to start off with a bang." She reached for a carton of orange juice. "By the way, how's this week's *Sixers* issue going?"

Amy sighed. "It's a lot more work than I realized," she answered. "I don't know how you did it all this time."

"I'm sure you can handle it," Elizabeth said. "You're an awesome editor and writer."

"Thanks," Amy said, stepping forward in the line. "That's because I had you as a teacher."

Elizabeth smiled. "I think it's more like we taught each other."

"Hey, it looks like Helen Bradley is trying to get your attention," Amy said.

Elizabeth looked over her shoulder and saw that, in fact, Helen Bradley, a seventh-grader with pretty red hair, *was* smiling at her and walking right toward her.

"Hi, Elizabeth. I was wondering if you'd like to sit at the table with me and my friends today," Helen said as she got closer. "We thought you might want to sit with your classmates."

Elizabeth smiled. *It's my first day and I'm already being asked to sit with other seventh-graders!* she thought. But she knew she couldn't just leave Amy. She and Amy had eaten lunch together almost every single day for as long as Elizabeth could remember. "Thanks for the offer, but I was going to sit with Amy," Elizabeth told Helen.

"Go ahead," Amy urged. "Helen's right. You should eat with other seventh-graders on your first day."

"Are you sure?" Elizabeth asked.

"Absolutely," Amy said firmly. "I'll talk to you later."

Elizabeth smiled at Helen, then followed her over to her table, where Leslie Carlisle and Kerry Glenn were sitting. Feeling the now-familiar combination of anxiety and excitement, she set down her tray.

"Hi, Jessica," Leslie said. "Welcome to the seventh grade."

Elizabeth felt her cheeks turn red. "Actually, I'm Elizabeth," she corrected. "Jessica's my identical twin sister. She's in the sixth grade."

"Oh, I see," Leslie said, looking across the room. Leslie was large-chested and very mature-looking.

"By the way, great shirt, Leslie," Kerry said. "Where'd you get it?"

"My sister drove me up the coast to a little boutique called Marla's," Leslie said, looking down at her yellow-and-pink checked midriff. "They have adorable things. Much hipper than anything you can find at the Sweet Valley Mall."

"Where do you buy your clothes, Elizabeth?" Kerry asked, glancing up and down at Elizabeth's white jeans and pink shirt with white flowers.

Elizabeth looked down at her outfit. *Maybe I should have borrowed something from Jessica,* she worried. Normally, she didn't spend all that much time on her clothes. This morning, she'd thought the outfit she'd chosen would make a good impression, but suddenly, she felt as if she had "I'm a sixth-grader" written all over her.

"I like to drive up the coast as well," Elizabeth answered before she knew what she was saying. "I mean, I like to have my mom drive me up the coast."

"Really? Which stores do you go to?" Leslie asked.

"Uh . . . Well, I guess my favorite store is . . . hmmm . . . I forget the name," Elizabeth fumbled.

As Leslie, Helen, and Kerry exchanged sly smiles, Elizabeth felt her face grow hot. *I should have known better than to lie,* she thought. *Obviously they can tell I never go shopping on the coast and that I have no idea what I'm talking about.* The truth was, Elizabeth never talked about shopping or clothes with her friends. That was Jessica's territory.

"Look, there's Gilda Samuels," Leslie said, putting her hand over her mouth to cover a giggle.

As everyone started to laugh hysterically, Elizabeth squirmed uncomfortably in her seat. She forced a weak giggle, even though she had no idea what the joke was.

"I still can't get that image from last Friday night out of my mind," Helen said.

"I know what you mean," Kerry said, shaking all over with laughter. "She looked like she was about to be sick or something when the bottle landed on her."

"She got hit with a bottle?" Elizabeth asked, trying to join in the conversation.

The girls all looked at one another again and laughed even harder.

"No, we were playing Spin the Bottle," Helen explained through her laughter.

"Oh, I see," Elizabeth said, forcing a smile. *What's Spin the Bottle?* she wondered, feeling that the girls might as well have been speaking a foreign language. There was obviously a lot she had to learn besides schoolwork.

As the girls at her table were giggling hysterically, Elizabeth glanced over at the table where Amy, Todd, Maria, and Winston were sitting. They all looked so comfortable with one another, and for a moment, Elizabeth wished she were sitting with them instead.

Then she shook the thought out of her head. *I just have to be patient. I'm sure I'll start to feel comfortable with these girls soon. I'll end up having a lot in common with them.*

Five

Hurry up and get here, Elizabeth, Jessica thought impatiently as she stared at the front door of Casey's, a popular ice cream parlor, waiting for her sister to show up. It was Thursday afternoon, and Jessica was sitting at a booth with Todd, Winston, Maria, and Amy.

"Have you guys decided what you're doing for your science projects?" Todd asked.

"I'm making up a model for a computer game," Winston said.

Winston was one of the best science students in the school, and Jessica and her friends thought he was a total geek. She never really understood why Elizabeth was such good friends with him—but then again, she never really understood why Elizabeth was friends with any of these dull people.

"I thought I'd do something that relates to the camping trip," Maria said. "Maybe something about the ecosystems."

Jessica drummed her fingers on the table. *This must be the most boring conversation in the history of the world*, she thought. She was dying to go hang out with the Unicorns, who were sitting at a booth across the ice cream parlor, but she had to stick around to make Elizabeth jealous.

Finally, after what seemed like an eternity, Elizabeth walked through the door and toward their booth with an enormous smile on her face.

"Wow, look out ladies and germs, Elizabeth Wakefield, the seventh-grader, is actually going to sit with us children," Winston teased.

Elizabeth slid into the booth. "Yes, I thought I could lower my standards for just this once. I hope nobody's watching, though."

"I think you're safe," Maria assured her, giggling.

"So, Jess, why aren't you sitting with the Unicorns?" Elizabeth asked.

"I was hoping to go over my article with Amy," Jessica said, beaming. "She's a great editor."

"Thanks, Jessica, but you're saying that to the expert editor," Amy said modestly.

"Well, let's hope the people at the *7&8 Gazette* see it the same way," Elizabeth said.

"I'm sure they'll be happy to have you on their paper," Todd said, patting Elizabeth on the back.

"Hey, Elizabeth," Tom McKay, a seventh-grader, said as he passed by their booth. "I hope I'm going to see you at my party tomorrow night."

Jessica felt her cheeks flush. *But I'm the one who's been dying to go to that party*, she thought miserably. *I'm the one who's a Unicorn and friends with Janet Howell!*

"I'd love to go," Elizabeth said enthusiastically.

"Great. See you then," Tom said as he walked to a booth in the back.

"Sorry, Jess," Elizabeth said with a sympathetic expression.

Jessica managed a blank look. "Sorry? What are you sorry about?"

Elizabeth raised her eyebrows. "Well, I know that you really wanted to go to that party."

"Oh, that," Jessica said, forcing a laugh and shrugging her shoulders. "Actually, I wouldn't go to Tom's tomorrow night if you paid me."

Elizabeth frowned. "But the other day you were saying that it would be the best party of the year."

Jessica waved her hand dismissively. "That was before I heard that it was supposed to be really boring."

"Why is it going to be boring?" Maria asked. "I always heard that seventh-and-eighth-grade parties were a lot of fun."

"Yeah, me too," Amy agreed.

"Ummm . . . well, they're going to just sit around and talk about boring things," Jessica said, trying to think fast. "They won't dance or anything like that."

"Boring things? What kind of boring things would they talk about?" Elizabeth asked.

"Oh, you know . . . just your typical boring things," Jessica answered vaguely.

Elizabeth laughed. "Well, you know how I usually like stuff that you find boring, so I'll probably have a great time."

"Yeah, you probably will," Jessica said, her face heating up. "You'll probably have a total blast."

*   *   *

Elizabeth was singing out loud as she set the table for dinner on Thursday night. Her first day of seventh grade had gone really well. She'd liked all of her classes and new teachers, and she was happy to have been invited to Tom's party.

Parties weren't exactly the center of her universe, but she thought going to Tom's party would give her the perfect chance to meet some seventh-graders. She looked forward to having more sophisticated conversations than she did with most sixth-graders—conversations about her favorite books and that sort of thing.

"Hey, Lizzie," Jessica said cheerfully as she walked into the kitchen. "Can I help you set the table?"

Elizabeth looked at her sister in surprise. "Let me get this straight. You're *offering* to help me with *my* chores? This has to be the first time in history."

"I guess it's because I'm in such a great mood," Jessica said, gleefully setting the plates around the table.

"Any particular reason?"

"I'm really excited about the camping trip," Jessica replied. "I just got off the phone with Todd, and we're going shopping with Amy and Maria this weekend for sleeping bags and everything."

"Sounds great," Elizabeth said, looking closely at Jessica. "It's funny—you seem to be spending more time with my friends than you are with the Unicorns."

"Well, now they're *my* friends, too. I'm glad I'm finally getting a chance to really know them," Jessica said, beaming. "Oh, by the way, if you want to borrow some of my clothes for the party tomorrow, feel free to look through my closet."

Elizabeth furrowed her brow. "Since when do you offer to lend *me* clothes? I'm always the one who has to hide my new clothes to keep you from taking them."

"Oh, I just figured you must be pretty nervous about what you're going to wear tomorrow night, since you don't want to make the *wrong* impression," Jessica said casually.

"What do you mean, 'the *wrong* impression'?" Elizabeth asked.

Jessica let out a laugh as if the answer were obvious. "You have to dress like a seventh-grader," she answered. "No offense, but if you walk through that door wearing what you usually do—like what you're wearing right now, for example—they'll probably laugh you right out of the house."

Elizabeth looked down at her outfit. She was wearing a button-down pink oxford shirt and khaki pants with white sneakers. "What's wrong with what I'm wearing?"

Jessica shrugged. "Well, nothing, I guess," she said, turning her attention back to the stack of plates in her hands. "Especially if you're going to a fourth-grade birthday party."

"What are you talking about?"

"You might as well face the facts, Lizzie," Jessica said, sighing. "That outfit is totally uncool for a seventh-and-eighth-grade party."

"But I like this outfit," Elizabeth protested.

"Suit yourself," Jessica said, shaking her head.

"Oh, and speaking of making the right impression, how are you wearing your hair?"

"I thought I'd just wear it in a ponytail like I always do," Elizabeth said uneasily, feeling her ponytail with her hand.

"Get real," Jessica said, rolling her eyes. "You really need to do something a little more sophisticated with it. *No* one will believe you're a seventh-grader if you wear a ponytail to a party. And are you getting someone to help you with your makeup?"

"You know I never wear makeup," Elizabeth said, laughing. "I think it's silly, and I'm still too young to wear it."

"Look," Jessica said, putting her hands on her hips, "if you're going to be a seventh-grader, you're going to have to start acting like one. You'll be the only girl there *not* wearing makeup."

Elizabeth sighed. "I guess I never thought about it, but going to a seventh-grade party really sounds like hard work. I wish you were coming with me. I *am* sorry that you weren't invited."

"Well, don't be," Jessica said firmly. "I'm just happy for you. It will be your big chance to make a good first impression on everyone—to show them that just because you're brand new to seventh grade and don't really know anyone and have never worn makeup or really mature clothes before, you're just as cool and sophisticated as they are."

"Uh, yeah," Elizabeth said in a soft voice. "Right."

"So did Elizabeth tell you about the seventh-and-eighth-grade party she's going to tomorrow night?"

Jessica asked her parents on Thursday night at dinner.

Out of the corner of her eye, Jessica noticed that Elizabeth was turning as red as the tomato sauce on her spaghetti.

"Elizabeth, is that true?" Mr. Wakefield asked as he exchanged concerned glances with Mrs. Wakefield. "Have you been invited to a party?"

Elizabeth cleared her throat. "Yes, it is. Tom McKay, this really nice guy in the seventh grade, is having the party at his house."

"And there won't be any sixth-graders there," Jessica interjected, ignoring Elizabeth's glare. "I'm sure it will be really fun," she continued breezily. "It will definitely be a lot more exciting than a sixth-grade party."

"I thought you said it was going to be boring," Elizabeth reminded her.

"Well, sure, a little bit, but it won't be *that* boring," Jessica said, gently kicking Steven under the table.

"I remember those parties from when I was in seventh and eighth grade," Steven said, not missing a beat. "They were pretty wild."

"What do you mean by 'wild'?" Mrs. Wakefield asked, frowning in concern.

"Well, let's just say they're a *lot* more interesting than sixth-grade parties," Steven said, shaking his head for emphasis. "One time, a bunch of the eighth-grade guys got together and . . ."

"What?" Mrs. Wakefield pressed, leaning forward.

"Maybe I shouldn't say," Steven said, letting out a big sigh. "I mean, that was a few years ago, and I'm sure the party Elizabeth's going to won't be like that."

"I don't know about this, Elizabeth," Mr. Wakefield said. "This sounds like it could be a little too advanced for you."

"But I *have* to go to this party," she pleaded. "I already told Tom I'd be there, and it's a great chance to really get to know other seventh-graders."

"She has a point," Jessica said, giving her sister a sympathetic look. "Plus, this party is going to be vital to her reputation. She'll be doomed to unpopularity if she doesn't go to the first party she's invited to. She has to prove to the seventh-graders that she's old enough to be in their class."

"That's certainly not a good reason for Elizabeth to go to the party," Mrs. Wakefield said sternly. "She'll have friends even if she doesn't go."

"Your mother's right," Mr. Wakefield said. "This is sounding more and more like a bad idea."

"But this party isn't going to be wild like that," Elizabeth said quickly. "Jessica, tell them about how you heard people were just going to be sitting around talking."

"Oh, I forgot to tell you," Jessica said, hitting her palm on her forehead. "Lila called this afternoon when I got home. She told me that it's going to be *tons* more exciting than I thought. They're going to be playing different games and stuff." She groaned dramatically. "I would absolutely *die* to go to this party. You're really lucky, Elizabeth. I mean, you were lucky to be invited."

"What kind of games are they going to be playing?" Mrs. Wakefield asked, furrowing her brow.

"I think I know the kind of games she's talking

about," Steven said. "And I don't think we want to talk about it at dinner."

As her parents exchanged a meaningful look, Jessica bit her lip to conceal her grin. Her plan was working perfectly.

"I'm sorry, honey," Mr. Wakefield said, turning to Elizabeth, "but your mother and I just don't think going to that party is a good idea."

Jessica turned to Elizabeth, who looked as though she was about to burst into tears. "Hey, Lizzie," she said sweetly, "I guess since you're not going to Tom's after all, you and I could do something fun instead— just the two of us."

"Yeah, maybe," Elizabeth muttered sadly.

Six

◇

"This journalism stuff is really great," Jessica said to Elizabeth and Steven on Thursday night. She was sprawled out on the floor of the family room, working on her article. Elizabeth was sitting on the couch, looking totally absorbed by the book she was reading, and Steven was sitting at the desk doing his math homework. "I wish I'd started working on the *Sixers* a long time ago."

"Hmm," Elizabeth mumbled, not looking up from her book.

"Working on this article is getting me more and more excited about the camping trip. For sixth-graders. Weekend after next," Jessica continued.

"Uh-huh," Elizabeth muttered.

"Of course, Amy was originally going to be doing the camping trip article, but now that she's editor-in-chief, she has too many responsibilities, so she assigned it to me," Jessica went on, waiting for

Elizabeth to start getting annoyed at her.

"Wow, that chapter was really fantastic," Elizabeth said, shutting her book. "I think this is going to be one of my favorite books of all time."

Jessica sighed in frustration. For some reason Elizabeth wasn't getting jealous of her.

"What book is it?" Steven asked, stretching his neck.

"*To Kill a Mockingbird*, by Harper Lee," Elizabeth answered.

"That's a great book," Steven agreed.

"Too bad we're not reading it at the same time," Jessica said to Elizabeth, sighing mournfully. "It's always fun to read the same book at the same time so we can talk about it together."

Elizabeth gave Jessica a quizzical look. "When did we ever do that?"

"Well . . . well, the point is, it *would* be a blast if we could read books we love at the same time, but now I guess we'll never have the chance." Jessica stared wistfully into space. "In fact, there are a lot of things we won't be able to do together anymore."

"Like what?" Elizabeth asked.

"Uh . . . well," Jessica stammered. "We won't be able to talk about our teachers with each other or help each other with our homework."

"We can still do that," Elizabeth pointed out. "We just won't have the same teachers or homework."

Jessica shook her head forlornly. "I'm sure you'll get so caught up with your new seventh-grade friends that you won't have time for me."

"That's never going to happen, and you know it,"

Elizabeth said. "You'll always be my twin sister and my best friend in the world."

"I hope you're right," Jessica said, smiling weakly. "And I hope that being in seventh grade doesn't *ruin* you."

Elizabeth frowned. "What do you mean, *'ruin'* me?"

"Well," Jessica said, "you're so innocent and friendly now. But seventh-graders can be so tough and mean—nice people just don't last long. Seventh grade will probably change you."

Elizabeth laughed. "I seriously doubt that seventh-graders are all that mean. They can't be too different from sixth-graders."

"Believe me, Elizabeth, take it from someone who's friends with seventh- and eighth-graders—they can be nasty," Jessica said knowingly. "Especially the girls. If they decide for some reason that they don't like you, they can make your life miserable. Right, Steven?"

"Actually, I think the guys are the worst," Steven replied. "They're the ones that could give you trouble."

"Oh, yeah, the guys," Jessica said, slapping her hand on her forehead. "That reminds me—Mary told me a story about a girl who was in the seventh grade and changed schools because of a party she went to."

Elizabeth frowned. "I never heard that before."

That's because it never happened, Jessica thought. "Yeah, well, it's not the sort of thing people talk about when they want to make polite conversation," she explained.

"So who was it?" Elizabeth asked.

"Missy Maples," Jessica replied instantly.

"Missy Maples?" Elizabeth repeated, looking puzzled. "I've never heard of her. Who was she?"

"Oh, just some girl," Jessica answered, waving her hands abstractedly.

"What I mean is, what happened to her?" Elizabeth pressed.

"What happened to her? Well, she . . . uh . . ." Jessica shot Steven a look.

"I think I heard about this," Steven cut in. "What happened was, Mamie went to this party—"

"I thought you said her name was Missy," Elizabeth interrupted.

"I did say that." Jessica raised her eyebrow at Steven.

"Right. Missy," Steven said, not skipping a beat. "So Missy went to a party one night, and when she got there, everyone was doing a certain kind of dance."

"Oh, yeah, now I remember," Jessica said excitedly. "Everyone was doing this dance, and Mandy—I mean Missy—didn't know how to do it."

"So everyone started making fun of her and laughing at her," Steven continued, "until she ran out of the house in tears."

"And when she went back to school on Monday, nobody would talk to her anymore," Jessica said, narrowing her eyes. "She changed schools a week later. Poor Mamie . . . I mean Missy."

Elizabeth looked at her brother and sister warily. "Well, if that actually happened, it *is* a terrible story," she said, picking up her book again. "But I'm sure nothing like that will happen to me—especially since

I'm not even allowed to go to Tom's party."

"Right," Jessica said. "Good thing you're not going. But you should still be careful. You never know what mean tricks seventh-graders will play on you."

"Mmm," Elizabeth mumbled, absorbed in her book.

"So are you psyched for tonight or what?" Leslie asked Kerry, Helen, and Elizabeth at lunch on Friday. Amy was spending the lunch period working on the *Sixers*, so Elizabeth decided to eat with the seventh-graders again.

"I can't wait," Helen said excitedly. "I just have to decide what to wear."

"I'm wearing that new pink blouse I bought at the mall last weekend," Leslie said. "It should look awesome with my jeans."

"What about you, Elizabeth?" Kerry asked. "What are you wearing?"

"I haven't decided yet," Elizabeth said uncomfortably. She couldn't admit the truth. Some of Jessica's warnings about seventh-graders seemed kind of fishy, but she was probably right about one thing—the girls would think she was a baby if they knew she wasn't allowed to go to her first seventh-grade party.

"Tom had a party a couple of months ago that was totally wild," Helen told her. "He always has the best parties."

"Hmm," Elizabeth mumbled.

"This will be a great chance for you to get to know some of the other kids in our class better," Kerry said to Elizabeth. "After tonight, you'll be a certified seventh-grader."

A certified seventh-grader. The words replayed in Elizabeth's head. She pictured herself at the party, surrounded by all her new classmates, laughing and talking about books and movies and that sort of thing.

She felt an overwhelming wave of frustration. *This is the best chance to really fit in as a seventh-grader, and I'm going to have to miss it.*

"You're really lucky to have such a great party to go to your first week as a seventh-grader," Leslie told Elizabeth. "Otherwise, it might be tough to really get to know people, since the year's already started, and everyone's into their own thing."

"Yeah," Elizabeth said, her cheeks burning. Suddenly, she couldn't stand it anymore. She had to go to that party—even if she had to sneak out to get there!

Am I losing my mind? Elizabeth thought as she walked home from school on Friday. Ever since lunch that day, she'd been feeling sick over the idea of lying to her parents and sneaking out to the party.

She turned the corner and started up her block, feeling a lump forming in her throat. *Mom and Dad would be so upset if they knew I was doing this*, she thought. *They've always trusted me.*

But the more she thought about what the girls had said at lunch—and what Jessica had said about looking like a baby—she realized she just didn't have a choice. It wasn't just about being popular—that had never really mattered to her. But even though making friends had always come easily to Elizabeth, she could tell that in seventh grade it would be hard work—as hard as any science quiz or English paper. And it seemed as though going to Tom's party was one of the assignments.

It looks like I won't have any friends if I don't go to this party, she reasoned as she kicked a pebble into the gutter. *And if I don't fit in socially as well as academically, I'm not a real seventh-grader.*

"Mom and Dad just left for their dinner party," Jessica said as she breezed into Elizabeth's room on Friday night. "I called Amy to tell her I wasn't coming over tonight, and I just ordered a pizza for you and me. I had them put extra cheese on your half."

Elizabeth pulled a T-shirt over her head and glanced at Jessica uneasily. "Thanks, Jess, that's really nice of you, but you might want to cancel that order. And you might want to call Amy back to tell her you're going over there after all."

"What are you talking about? I thought you *loved* extra cheese," Jessica protested.

"Yeah, extra cheese is great," Elizabeth agreed. "But it turns out I'm going to Tom's party."

"What?" Jessica gasped. "How could Mom and Dad change their minds just like that?"

Elizabeth turned to the mirror so she wouldn't have to face her sister. "Um, actually, they haven't. They don't know I'm going," she said under her breath. Just saying those words made her feel queasy.

"*What?*" Jessica asked.

"Don't make me repeat it, Jess," Elizabeth replied.

"Elizabeth! What's happening to you?" Jessica plopped down on Elizabeth's bed, her mouth open wide.

"Nothing's happening to me," Elizabeth said defensively. "*You're* the one who said how bad it would look if I didn't go to the first seventh-grade party I was invited to."

"But—but how could you totally do the opposite of what Mom and Dad told you to do?" Jessica asked in disbelief.

"Oh, look who's talking," Elizabeth snapped. "You always do the opposite of what Mom and Dad tell you to do. And you know you'd do the same thing in a blink of an eye if the situation were reversed."

"Well . . . uh . . . well, I'm not you," Jessica protested. "This isn't the kind of thing that you do."

Elizabeth sighed exhaustedly. *I'm not going to let her make me feel guilty. I'm not going to let her make me feel guilty,* she repeated to herself.

"Look, I'm going, and that's that," Elizabeth said flatly.

"You'll get in big trouble," Jessica cautioned.

"I won't if they don't find out," Elizabeth said, clenching her jaw. "And you're not going to tell them."

"Of course I won't," Jessica said, folding her arms. "What kind of a sister do you think I am, anyway?"

Elizabeth gave Jessica a long, hard look and then turned back to the mirror.

After a few moments of tense silence, Jessica finally spoke. "Well, please tell me that's not what you're wearing. You look like a big green bean."

Elizabeth frowned at her reflection. She was now wearing a green T-shirt with green jeans and a matching green headband. "I guess I do look a little too green," she said with a sigh.

"Hold on, I'll be right back," Jessica said as she jumped up from the bed.

As she examined the contents of her closet, Elizabeth felt her stomach rumble with dread. *Jessica's right—all my clothes are totally babyish. What if I'm totally laughed out of the party?*

"OK, here are some different possibilities," Jessica announced as she came back into the room, carrying a huge stack of clothes. She spread the clothes out on the bed and held up a super-short, purple miniskirt. Purple was the official color of the Unicorn Club, so Jessica had a lot of purple clothing. "I think this would be the perfect thing for you."

"You must be kidding," Elizabeth said, laughing.

"I'm totally serious," Jessica insisted. "You would be totally cool in this skirt. You'd be the hit of the party."

"I think I'd look like a big idiot in that," Elizabeth said. "That's just not me, Jess."

"No offense, but maybe you don't want to be you tonight," Jessica said. "I mean, you're great and everything, but if you want to be accepted by the older kids, you're going to have to act like one and look like one."

"I've never seen anyone in the seventh grade wear a skirt like that before," Elizabeth pointed out.

"You've never been to one of their parties before,"

Jessica said knowingly. "Their party clothes are totally different from their school clothes. Everybody knows that."

"Well, I'm not wearing that skirt," Elizabeth said.

"Then try this on," Jessica said, handing her a pink halter dress. "I think this would look great with your coloring."

Elizabeth scrunched up her face and looked at the dress. "No way. That's for someone much older than me."

Jessica let out an exasperated sigh. "Don't you get it? That's the whole point. You *want* to look older than you are."

"Well, yes, but . . . No . . . I don't know," Elizabeth groaned.

"Look, Elizabeth, it's obvious that going to seventh-grade parties doesn't come naturally to you," Jessica said bluntly. "So maybe you should just quit trying to be something you're not and stay home with me instead."

Elizabeth rolled her eyes. "I'm going to this party, Jess."

"OK," Jessica said, looking down at the floor. "I can understand that the party would be a lot more fun than staying home with me."

"*Please* don't do this, Jessica," Elizabeth begged. Jessica was being kind of a pain, but Elizabeth hated to see her so sad—especially since Elizabeth was so frazzled to begin with. "I'd love to hang out with you and watch movies, but going to this party is just something I have to do. And thanks for the clothing advice, but I think I'll just go in jeans."

Jessica reached into the pile and pulled out a denim miniskirt. "This is really much more sophisticated than regular jeans."

"Fine," Elizabeth said, not wanting to argue anymore. She pulled her long-sleeved, purple-and-white striped T-shirt over her head.

"That's a dorky shirt, if you ask me," Jessica said as she took different kinds of makeup out of a small pink bag.

"Well, I like it," Elizabeth said firmly. "And I'm not wearing any of that stuff, so just put it back in the bag."

Jessica crossed her arms in front of her. "You're really being stubborn," she said. "I'm starting to think you don't want to have any friends."

"I do want to have friends," Elizabeth said, feeling more and more frustrated. "I just don't see how wearing makeup will help."

"It's nice that you're so confident, but I think you should listen to me," Jessica said. "I'm the one with friends in the seventh grade, after all. And I happen to know that none of them would be caught dead without their makeup on at a party."

Elizabeth looked at the different makeup items that were lying on the bed.

"OK," Elizabeth said reluctantly. "I'll wear a teeny, tiny little bit. But I don't want it to even look like I'm wearing any."

"I'm really trying not to lose my patience," Jessica said, throwing her hands up in the air. "What's the point in wearing makeup if you don't want people to be able to tell that you're wearing any?"

Elizabeth glanced at the digital clock by her bed and saw that it was seven thirty—thirty minutes before the party was supposed to start. "Look, Mary Wallace's parents are going to be here soon to pick me up, so just put it on, but don't overdo it."

"That's more like it," Jessica said. "Sit down."

Elizabeth sat down in front of her dresser and closed her eyes. She couldn't bear to watch.

After a few minutes, Jessica told Elizabeth to open her eyes.

"Oh, no!" Elizabeth gasped when she looked in the mirror. "I look like a clown!" There was blue eye shadow smeared all over her eyelids and red lipstick coming off the sides of her lips.

"What are you talking about? You look beautiful."

Elizabeth grabbed a tissue and started wiping her face. "I'll be the laughingstock of the party!"

"Don't wipe it off," Jessica said, grabbing the tissue from Elizabeth. "You'll just make it worse."

Elizabeth looked again in the mirror. Jessica was right—she really looked silly now. She had smeared makeup all over her face, and the more she tried to take it off, the messier it got.

"What am I going to do?" Elizabeth asked desperately. "I can't go to the party like this."

Jessica ran to the closet and grabbed a baseball hat. "Put this hat on for the car ride with Mary and her parents. I'll ask them if they'll drop me off at Amy's, and we'll bring some tissues in the car. We'll sit in the backseat, and I'll help you clean up some of this awful mess you made."

"Good idea," Elizabeth said frantically.

"I'll meet you downstairs in ten minutes," Jessica said. "There's something I have to do first."

"Where's the number Mom and Dad left us?" Jessica asked breathlessly as she bounded into the family room where Steven was watching television.

"What number?" Steven asked, barely taking his eyes off the TV.

"You know," she said quickly. "The number of the people whose house they're eating at."

"It's right there by the phone," Steven said. "Why? What's up?"

"You're not going to believe it," Jessica said as she picked up the receiver. "Elizabeth's sneaking off to go to the party. When Mom and Dad find out, they'll go ballistic. They'll insist that she go back to the sixth grade *immediately*."

"I wouldn't call them if I were you," Steven said casually.

"Are you nuts? This is the moment I've been waiting for," Jessica said.

Steven shook his head. "Think about it, Jessica. Mom and Dad are too proud of Elizabeth to send her back to sixth grade. They'll probably just ground her or something. But if Elizabeth is so dead set on going to the party, we should let her—it might be just what she needs to realize she's not ready for the seventh-grade scene."

Jessica thought for a minute and looked back down at the phone. "Hmmm . . . maybe you have a point." She glanced at Steven and frowned. "By the way, why are you being so helpful lately?"

"Because I enjoy proving to you that I'm always right," he answered simply.

Jessica rolled her eyes. "Sorry I asked."

Seven

"Did your parents say you needed to be home by a special time?" Mrs. Wallace asked Elizabeth when she slid next to Jessica in the backseat of the Wallaces' car. Mary Wallace was a seventh-grader and one of the only Unicorns who was friends with both Jessica and Elizabeth.

"Oh, no," Elizabeth answered softly, looking down at the carpeting on the floor. "I'll just go whenever Mary's ready."

This is unbelievable—not only is Elizabeth doing this behind Mom and Dad's back, but now she's lying to Mary's mother too! Jessica thought. *I'm the one who's supposed to be pulling this kind of thing—not Elizabeth. Seventh grade has really changed her.*

"How do I look?" Elizabeth whispered to Jessica, who was wiping off her makeup while Mary talked to her mother.

"Beautiful," Jessica told her. In fact, Elizabeth

didn't look all that beautiful. The makeup didn't seem to be coming off, and it was so smudged that Elizabeth really *did* look like a clown.

"I'm so nervous and excited I can barely breathe," Elizabeth whispered as she twisted a strand of hair around her finger.

Jessica felt a slight twinge of guilt. She knew she should let Elizabeth know what her face looked like, but she just couldn't bring herself to. *If she walks in that party looking like that, she'll definitely be laughed out the door.*

"Tell me again why you're going to Amy's house, Jessica," Mary said. "I never knew you were such good friends with her."

"I'm realizing I really have lots in common with her," Jessica replied. "Tonight it'll be sort of a mini-party. Todd and Maria are coming over, and we're going to plan the camping trip and order Chinese food together. It should be a blast."

This will probably be the most devastatingly boring evening of my life, Jessica said to herself. She was spending so much time with Elizabeth's friends lately that she was afraid that even *she* was becoming a duller person. *But if things go the way I think they're going to, Elizabeth will be running back to sixth grade faster than I can say "makeup,"* Jessica thought. *Then I can lose those boring people for good.*

"OK, Mary and Elizabeth," Mrs. Wallace said as they pulled up in front of Tom's house. "You just give me a call when you're ready to leave."

"Do you really think I look like I'm going to fit in?" Elizabeth whispered to Jessica as she got out of the car.

"Of course you will, Lizzie," Jessica said, giving her sister a comforting pat on the shoulder and taking her baseball cap. "Just be yourself."

When she and Mary reached the McKays' front door, Elizabeth drew in a deep breath and reached for the doorbell. Before her finger actually touched it, she caught a glimpse of herself in the window to the side of the door. *Oh, my gosh! I look like a joke! How could Jessica let me out of the car looking like this?*

"Mary, you go on inside," Elizabeth said. "I'll be there in a minute."

"Are you sure?" Mary asked. "Is something wrong?"

"No, everything's fine," Elizabeth lied, looking down so Mary wouldn't see her face. "I just have to do something."

Elizabeth ran around to the side of the house, making sure nobody had seen her. She spotted the outside spigot for the hose and turned it on. Luckily, she'd had some tissues in her pocket. She washed off her face so thoroughly that she was sure she'd removed every trace of the makeup.

She walked back up to the front of the house and looked in the window again. *Phew!* The makeup seemed to be completely gone. Her heart pounding, she rang the doorbell.

"Hey, Wakefield," Tom said as he opened the door. "Glad you could make it."

"Thanks," Elizabeth said, feeling the butterflies in her stomach start to flap their wings around even harder. "It's nice to be here. Thanks for inviting me."

"Sure thing," Tom said. "Why don't you come on in and get yourself something to eat and drink. We've got burgers and hot dogs out in the backyard and about ten different kinds of sodas and chips."

"Sounds good," Elizabeth said awkwardly.

Elizabeth walked out to the backyard, where everyone was standing around in small groups. She spotted Helen, Kerry, and Leslie standing in a circle with three other girls whom she didn't know. *Just go for it*, she told herself. *They invited me to eat lunch with them two days in a row, so they must like me a little bit. Be calm and be yourself.*

"Hi, guys," Elizabeth said casually, as if she went to parties like this all the time. "Nice party."

"Hey, Elizabeth," Helen said coolly. Leslie and Kerry gave her a tight smile.

Well, it's not the biggest welcome in the world, but maybe this is just how seventh-graders act at parties, Elizabeth reasoned.

"I heard Peter and Sara are breaking up," Leslie said to the group. "Apparently, they got in a huge fight the other day. In fact, Sara was so mad at Peter that she didn't even come to the party tonight, since he was going to be here."

"What was their fight about?" Elizabeth asked.

"I don't know," Leslie said. "But I hear it was pretty wretched."

This isn't so bad, Elizabeth thought with relief. *At least they're including me in their conversation.*

"Look at Debbie," Leslie said, pointing to a brown-haired girl on the other side of the lawn who was surrounded by a group of guys. "She's up to her usual tricks again."

"What are her usual tricks?" Elizabeth asked, trying to participate in the discussion.

"Debbie's this huge flirt," Helen said. "She doesn't have any girlfriends because all she cares about is guys."

Elizabeth felt sorry for Debbie. *Everybody should have a girlfriend*, she thought. Elizabeth noticed how Debbie kept looking over at the group of girls Elizabeth was standing with as if she wanted to join them. *She'd probably love to come over here, but she knows they wouldn't be that nice to her.*

"So which games do you think we're going to play tonight?" Helen asked, smiling slyly.

"We'll just have to wait and see," Leslie said, giving Helen a look Elizabeth couldn't interpret.

Elizabeth felt a flicker of excitement. She had no idea what kind of games people played at parties like this, but she was good at games—she'd probably really like that part of the party.

"OK, Jessica, do you have any suggestions about activities we should do on the camping trip?" Amy asked.

Jessica was sitting on Amy's living room floor with Elizabeth's boring friends, eating Chinese food.

"Yeah, I think someone should bring a boom box and we can have a dance contest," Jessica suggested.

Amy, Maria, Todd, and Winston looked at her as if she'd just suggested they fly to the moon.

"You're kidding, right?" Winston asked.

"No, I'm not," Jessica said defensively. "I think it would be a blast to dance outside around the campfire."

"Jessica," Amy started gently, "I think you're kind of missing the point of the camping trip."

"I thought the point was to have fun," Jessica said, putting her hands on her hips.

"Well, it is," Amy said. "But I think we're supposed to have fun in a more nature-related way."

Nature-related? Jessica thought. *Where are these people from? Mars?*

"I think we should have a nature treasure hunt," Maria said excitedly.

"That's a great idea," Todd agreed.

"Everyone could have a list of different kinds of things they should collect," Maria explained. "Like, different kinds of plant leaves and insects . . ."

"Insects?" Jessica gasped. "Gross!"

"Well, it is a camping trip," Todd reminded her. "It's not like we're going to be staying in a luxury hotel or anything."

Duh, Jessica felt like saying. "I know that," she said in a prickly voice. "But I, for one, am not going to be picking up any bugs."

"I think we should make a list of songs to sing around the campfire," Amy said.

"I'll make the list," Jessica volunteered. "Johnny Buck has some great songs on his latest CD." Johnny Buck was Jessica's favorite rock star, and she had every CD he ever recorded.

"Jessica, I don't think that's the kind of thing Amy had in mind," Maria said.

"No, I was thinking more of traditional camp songs," Amy said. "You know, like 'Kumbaya' and 'He's Got the Whole World in His Hands' and stuff."

"You mean, those baby songs?" Jessica said, rolling her eyes.

"I don't think they're babyish," Amy protested.

"Me neither," Maria said.

Jessica raised her eyebrows at Todd and Winston.

"I love those songs," Winston said.

"Same here," Todd agreed.

These really are the dullest people in the world, Jessica thought, shaking her head in disbelief. *How can Elizabeth stand spending so much time with them?*

This is going to be a weird game, Elizabeth thought as she joined the circle of kids sitting on the floor of Tom's living room. *The only game I can think of where we sit in a circle is Duck Duck Goose.*

Elizabeth was sitting between Mary and Kerry, but she was too embarrassed to ask them what kind of game they were playing. She seemed to be the only one who didn't know what was going on.

Everyone seemed to be giddy with excitement over the soda bottle that was lying in the middle of the circle. Elizabeth remembered a conversation about bottles at lunch that week, but she had no idea what they'd been talking about.

"I hope it lands on Rick Hunter when it's my turn," Kerry whispered to Elizabeth.

Elizabeth just smiled and nodded. *What is she talking about? Is everyone going to take turns throwing the bottle at one another?*

Tom picked up the bottle and looked around the circle. "Hmm, who should go first?" His eyes fell on Elizabeth. "OK, Wakefield, you're up."

Tom walked over to her and handed her the bottle. She stared at it for a second, then looked at Tom. "What am I supposed to do with this?" she asked timidly.

Elizabeth thought she heard quiet snickering around the room. Obviously, she had asked the wrong question.

"You put the bottle in the middle of the circle and spin it around," Tom explained.

"Is that all?" Elizabeth asked.

"That'll do for starters," Tom said with a huge grin on his face.

Elizabeth leaned forward and spun the bottle. *This is pretty silly*, she thought. *What's the point?* She watched as the bottle spun around and slowly came to a stop.

"Way to go, Bruce!" some of the guys shouted. Others whistled, and most of the girls giggled.

Elizabeth looked at Bruce Patman, who was smiling mischievously back at her. Bruce Patman was an eighth-grader and one of the best-looking and wealthiest guys in the school. Both Elizabeth and Jessica thought he was also one of the most *obnoxious* guys in the school.

What happens now? she wondered. *Am I supposed to throw the bottle at him or something?*

Bruce stood up and walked toward Elizabeth. *What's going on? Why is he coming over here?* She had a funny feeling she wasn't going to like whatever was going to happen next.

Before she knew what was going on, Bruce was sitting down in front of her, craning his face toward hers. When she saw him pucker up his lips, she thought she was going to faint. *I'm supposed to kiss him,* she realized in horror. She looked around at all the expectant faces, then back at Bruce.

Just as Bruce was about to plant his lips on top of her own, she quickly turned her face so that the kiss landed on her cheek.

"Hey, what's the big idea?" Bruce asked in an exasperated tone. "Don't you know how to play this game?"

The whole room erupted in laughter. Elizabeth was paralyzed. She opened her mouth, but she couldn't say anything. Tears began to form in her eyes.

"What a baby," Janet Howell said from across the room.

"She belongs in the fourth grade," Kimberly Haver, a seventh-grade Unicorn, added.

"I'm sorry I didn't tell you what was going to happen," Mary whispered to her. "I guess I thought you knew."

"That's OK," Elizabeth mumbled. "Excuse me."

She stood up and walked quickly out of the room and into the bathroom, where she let the tears finally flow down her face. *Why didn't somebody warn me seventh grade would be like this?* she thought miserably. Then she realized that people did warn her—Jessica, Steven, and even her parents. No one thought she would be able to handle it—and here she was, proving them right. Looking at her tearstained reflection in the mirror, Elizabeth suddenly felt angry with herself for being so easily defeated.

I can't let this get me down, she told herself as she splashed cold water on her face. *I have to go back in there and show them that I'm a real seventh-grader.*

"OK, almost everyone's had a turn," Janet Howell announced twenty minutes after Elizabeth had come back to the circle. "Let's play Truth or Dare."

Elizabeth took a deep breath to calm her nerves. She had heard of Truth or Dare, but she'd never played it before. Even though she still felt awful about that whole kissing incident, she was determined to stick out a second game. After all, if she was going to make it as a seventh-grader, she had to do more than just get good grades.

They took turns going around the circle, and after a few minutes it was Helen's turn.

"Truth or dare?" Tom asked her.

"I'll take a truth," Helen said, looking totally calm and cool.

"OK," Tom said, furrowing his brow in deep thought. "Who did you really want the bottle to land on when it was your turn?"

Helen giggled and smiled broadly. "Rick Hunter," she announced loudly.

Everyone started making whooping sounds, and a couple of guys patted Rick on the back. Elizabeth squirmed uncomfortably. *I'd die if I had to announce something like that.*

Tom looked at her. "It's your turn, Wakefield."

Elizabeth's pulse was racing. She felt about forty eyes all looking at her at the same time.

"OK, Elizabeth, truth or dare?" Janet asked her.

"I don't care," she answered softly, not knowing which would be worse.

"If you don't care, I'll decide for you—you're doing a dare," Tom said.

"I really don't think you want to do a dare that Janet decides," Mary cautioned Elizabeth.

"Really?" Elizabeth asked nervously.

"Really," Mary said, nodding her head. "Let's just get out of here. I'll call my mom and we can wait outside. The party's almost over, anyway."

Elizabeth hesitated for a moment. She didn't want to look as if she was chickening out, but given how the last game turned out, maybe it would be better if she just left now. At least she had stayed for a little bit of this game. She nodded at Mary. "OK, I'm ready to go."

Mary stood up instantly. "Elizabeth and I have to go now," she announced.

"You're leaving right in the middle of your dare?" Janet asked, looking at Elizabeth disapprovingly.

"Those are the breaks," Mary said quickly. "Let's go, Elizabeth."

"I have an idea," Janet said as Elizabeth and Mary started to leave. "I'll think about what your dare should be over the weekend, and you'll have to do whatever it is in school next week."

"That's fine," Elizabeth said quickly as she headed to the door. At that point, she really couldn't care less about what happened next week. All she knew was that she wanted out of that house as soon as possible.

*   *   *

They're back! Elizabeth thought as soon as Mary's mother dropped her off and she saw her parents' car in the driveway. *Now I'll be grounded for the rest of my life!*

But she felt a strange wave of relief at being caught. *At least now I won't have to go to any more parties like that.* She walked slowly through the front door and prepared herself for the worst.

"Hi, honey," Mrs. Wakefield called out from the living room.

Elizabeth took a deep breath and entered the room. *This is it. I'm just going to confess everything and take my punishment.*

"Hi, Mom," she muttered weakly, relieved to see that her father wasn't there. Having both of them scold her at the same time would be worse.

"Did you have fun tonight?" Mrs. Wakefield asked, smiling.

Elizabeth felt the color drain from her face. Did her mother know where she was tonight?

Her mother smiled at Elizabeth's expression. "Jessica told us you were at Amy's with her and decided to stay a little longer. We called to see when we could pick you up, and Amy's mother told us that you weren't there. So we finally got Jessica to tell us the truth—that you went to the party after all."

Elizabeth gasped. Even though Mrs. Wakefield didn't seem the least bit angry, Elizabeth felt terrible that her parents had to find out the truth this way. "Mom, I'll never—"

"Actually, sweetheart, there's something I wanted to tell you," Mrs. Wakefield interrupted, putting her arm around Elizabeth's shoulders. "It was wrong of you to sneak out to the party tonight, but—"

"I know," Elizabeth cut in, "and I'll never—"

Mrs. Wakefield held up her hand. "But I think I know why you did it."

"You do?" Elizabeth asked timidly.

Mrs. Wakefield nodded. "I know how much you wanted to go to that party tonight," she continued sweetly. "Well, your father and I discussed it, and we decided that it was wrong of us not to let you go. We know that fitting in socially is just as important as succeeding academically. And we don't want anything to ruin your experience as a seventh-grader."

"You don't?" Elizabeth asked softly.

Her mother shook her head. "You're making us so happy. We know how hard you've been working. This must be a difficult adjustment for you, and we want to help you out in any way we can. So we're allowing you to go to the next party you're invited to."

"You are?" Elizabeth asked, her heart sinking.

Her mother nodded, smiling warmly.

"You guys must, um, really want me to make it as a seventh-grader," Elizabeth said, practically in a whisper.

"Of course we do, sweetheart," her mother said, kissing her on the forehead. "I'm so proud of you!"

"Thanks, Mom," Elizabeth said, smiling weakly. She was having trouble breathing. *There's no turning back now*, she realized for the first time. *Mom would be heartbroken if it turned out I wasn't up to the seventh grade.*

Eight

◇

"So tell me everything!" Jessica said to Elizabeth on Saturday morning. Jessica was sunbathing by the pool in the Wakefields' backyard. Elizabeth was sitting at a table doing homework, and to Jessica's great pleasure, she didn't look too happy.

"It was fabulous," Elizabeth said, looking up from her enormous textbook. "In fact, it was the best party I've ever been to."

"It was?" Jessica asked.

"Yeah, it was perfect," Elizabeth gushed. "Everyone was really nice and cool."

"And did anyone say anything about your makeup?" Jessica asked.

"Oh, you mean about how it was smeared all over my face?" Elizabeth asked.

Jessica blushed and glanced at Elizabeth, who seemed to be giving her a funny look.

Elizabeth didn't wait for her to answer. "Actually,

no one mentioned it, because luckily I washed it all off before I went inside."

"Oh," Jessica said in a small voice. She cleared her throat. "So what did you do at the party?"

"Well, we talked and ate burgers and stuff, and then we played some really cool games," Elizabeth said.

"Games? Like what kind of games?" Jessica asked.

"Oh, you'll find out when you're in seventh grade," Elizabeth said casually.

Jessica felt a surge of anger. *Why is she rubbing it in that she's in the seventh grade and I'm not?*

"I had a great time last night too," Jessica lied. "It's too bad you weren't there. You would have had fun."

"What did you do?" Elizabeth asked.

"Well, first of all, Todd is such a funny guy," Jessica said. "He's always making these great jokes. I was dying from laughing so hard."

Elizabeth frowned. "Really? I mean, I think Todd's a fantastic guy, but I never thought of him as telling a lot of jokes and stuff."

"Well, maybe you just don't know that side of his personality," Jessica said airily. "And Amy's really great. We're talking about maybe sharing a tent together with Maria."

"What about your own friends, like Lila? Don't you want to share a tent with them?" Elizabeth asked, her brow furrowed.

"Maybe Lila will be in the tent with us too," Jessica replied.

"Lila would share a tent with Amy and Maria?" Elizabeth asked, frowning. "That's even weirder than *your* sharing one with them."

"I don't think it's weird at all," Jessica said, even though she thought it was the weirdest thing she'd ever heard. Lila thought that Amy and Maria were about as interesting as math class. "By the way, I'm going to the mall with Maria and Amy to look for sleeping bags, and then I'm meeting up with some of the Unicorns there this afternoon. Do you want to come?"

"I'd love to, but I have too much work to do," Elizabeth said, turning back to her book. "I think I'll be studying all day."

"That's too bad," Jessica said. "I feel like we never get to see each other anymore."

"Sure we do," Elizabeth argued. "And once I get caught up with all this work, I'll have a lot more free time."

"I hope so. Because if all you do is study, people will just start to forget about you, and pretty soon you'll have no more friends," Jessica said, closing her eyes and feeling the sun shine on her skin.

"How was your sister feeling this morning?" Mary asked Jessica on Saturday afternoon.

"She seemed fine," Jessica answered as they walked into Bibi's, one of her favorite clothing stores. She was thrilled to be with the Unicorns. Shopping with Amy and Maria earlier that day had been torture. They didn't want to shop for clothes, and all they talked about was what books they were reading. "Why do you ask?"

"Didn't she tell you what happened last night?" Janet asked, laughing.

"She just said she had a good time at the party," Jessica replied.

Mary and Janet exchanged knowing glances and Janet explained what had happened during the Spin the Bottle game.

So she was lying, Jessica thought. *She wanted me to think everything was cool, when really she totally humiliated herself!*

"And I'm in charge of coming up with a dare for Elizabeth to do in school next week," Janet said, smiling slyly as she pulled a purple-and-white polka dot dress off the rack.

Lila giggled. "You're going to have her do something *interesting,* I hope."

"Oh, I haven't figured it out yet, but it'll definitely be something *quite* interesting," Janet agreed.

"I think you should make it easy, considering what she went through last night," Mary said.

Jessica's mind was whirling. She knew that Mary was right—Elizabeth was humiliated enough already. But a part of her wanted to see Elizabeth humiliated even further—after all, this was a great opportunity to really push Elizabeth over the edge and send her running back to sixth grade.

As she looked through a rack of blouses, Jessica tried desperately to think of a good dare for Elizabeth. *What would she absolutely despise? What dare would be so horrible that Elizabeth would realize once and for all that she belongs in sixth grade?* Suddenly, Jessica broke into a wide grin.

"I have it!" she announced.

"You have what?" Mary asked, frowning at the

blouse Jessica was holding. "I think that's too frilly for you, Jessica."

"No, not this," Jessica said, putting the blouse back. "I mean, I know a good dare for Elizabeth!"

"What?" Janet asked, looking interested.

"*Well*, since she didn't kiss Bruce the way she was supposed to at the party last night, that should be her dare! She should have to kiss him in front of the whole school, in a public place like in the lunchroom." Jessica was so excited, she could barely contain herself. She thought her idea was brilliant. Not only did Elizabeth hate Bruce Patman, she would be mortified to have to kiss him in front of her teachers, friends, and especially Todd.

"Very impressive, Jessica," Janet said approvingly.

Jessica blushed. The Unicorn president's praise made her feel even more brilliant.

"I think it's really mean," Mary said. "Elizabeth would be totally embarrassed and upset. I think you should come up with something else."

Jessica felt a pang of guilt—her least favorite emotion. *Maybe it's a little mean, but this is for Elizabeth's own good*, she reasoned. Obviously, Elizabeth didn't belong in seventh grade, and last night proved it.

"Well, I think it sounds perfect," Janet said. "I can't wait to see it with my own eyes."

"That makes two of us," Jessica said.

Seventh grade is getting easier every day, Elizabeth thought as she sat in math class on Monday morning. *The schoolwork is, anyway*. It didn't seem fair that as soon as she was starting to master her schoolwork, things seemed to be getting worse for her on the social front.

Ever since Friday night, she'd been going over the events of Tom's party in her mind. She felt bad for lying to Jessica about what had really happened at the party, but she just couldn't tell her the truth. She didn't want to give Jessica any more reason to think she was too unsophisticated for the seventh grade.

"Elizabeth?" Ms. Larson called, startling Elizabeth out of her thoughts. "Would you like to take a stab at the problem up at the board?"

The classroom was completely quiet, and Elizabeth could almost hear her own heart beating. But as nervous as she was to do a math problem in front of the whole class, she was excited by the challenge. "Yes, ma'am," she said to her teacher, trying to sound confident and eager.

She walked to the front of the classroom and picked up a piece of chalk. *Stay calm*, she told herself. *You know this material.* After a couple of minutes of deep concentration, she started to write down different numbers on the board. Before she knew it, the problem was solved, and Ms. Larson was standing next to her, smiling her approval.

"That was absolutely perfect," Ms. Larson said. "You've obviously been studying a lot. I'm very impressed."

Elizabeth was elated. This was the moment she'd been waiting for. All the hard work she'd been doing over the past few days was finally paying off. And all the problems she'd been having with the social scene seemed miles away. *I love being in the seventh grade*, she thought happily.

"Do you want to try the next one?" Ms. Larson asked. "It's a little bit harder."

"I'll give it a try," Elizabeth said.

Elizabeth looked at the problem Ms. Larson had written on the board and took a deep breath. It *was* harder than the first problem, and Elizabeth wasn't sure she'd be able to do it. She could feel all the students watching her from behind. She picked up the chalk and started to write a couple of numbers. Soon, her hands were moving quickly, and the problem was solved.

"Great job," Ms. Larson said. "Keep up the good work."

Elizabeth floated back to her desk, feeling as if she were ten feet above the ground. She couldn't remember the last time she'd felt so proud.

As she walked out of her math class, Elizabeth spotted Helen, Kerry, and Leslie, standing around their lockers. *OK, just walk up to them and be yourself.*

"Hi, guys," Elizabeth said cheerfully as she approached them. "What's up?"

Everyone said hi back, but Elizabeth was getting the feeling that she was interrupting something.

"Too bad you missed the rest of Tom's party," Leslie said. "Things got more interesting after you left."

"Why *did* you leave so early?" Kerry asked. "Do you have a bedtime or something?"

Elizabeth flushed. "Actually, I had another party to go to," she said quickly, before she knew what she was saying. *I can't believe how much I've been lying lately. I'm acting less and less like myself,* she thought.

"Really?" Helen asked, obviously impressed. "Whose party?"

"Well, uh . . . it was a party that a friend of mine from another school was having," Elizabeth said. "It was really fun. We played Spin the Bottle and stuff."

"What school does your friend go to?" Leslie asked.

"She goes to Valley Friends," Elizabeth said.

"I know a lot of people who go there," Kerry said. "Who's your friend?"

"Sally Cassidy," she answered. The lies were coming more and more quickly.

"I've never heard of her," Kerry said. "I'll ask my friends if they know her."

I wish you wouldn't, Elizabeth thought. She cleared her throat. "So what did I miss at the party?" she asked, anxious to change the subject.

"Well, there were some really good dares," Helen said, her big blue eyes widening. "Kimberly Haver had to call the Hairnet on the phone and pretend like she was selling encyclopedias."

"So what happened?" Elizabeth asked, feigning enormous interest.

"The Hairnet actually placed an order for a whole set," Helen said, bursting into laughter. "She gave her credit card number to Kimberly and everything."

"Wow," Elizabeth said, trying to sound as though that were the coolest thing she'd ever heard. "What else?"

"Well, Maggie Sullivan had to kiss Duncan Saunders on the lips," Leslie said. "Can you imagine?

He's practically the ugliest guy in the school. I don't even know why Tom invited him to his party in the first place."

"Gross," Elizabeth said, scrunching up her face as if she'd eaten something sour. The truth was that Elizabeth actually *liked* Duncan, and she felt awful that the girls were making fun of him. *But am I any better? I'm not exactly rushing to his defense.*

"I gotta go," Elizabeth said. "I'll see you later."

Elizabeth walked away, feeling sick to her stomach. *Why am I trying so hard to fit in with girls who just aren't very nice?* she wondered.

Nine

◇

"So how are you liking your new job as editor-in-chief, Amy?" Elizabeth asked as she spread mustard on her hamburger. It was lunchtime on Monday, and Elizabeth was thrilled to be sitting with Amy and Maria again. She didn't have to worry about how she talked or dressed or acted—she could just be herself.

"I'm actually a little overwhelmed," Amy admitted as she squirted ketchup on her french fries. "I didn't realize how much work it was going to be. It'll be tough to get everything together by our deadline."

Elizabeth felt a wave of longing. She always loved the way she'd felt in the office the day before a deadline. The pace was hectic, but she liked having so much responsibility on her shoulders.

She smiled at Amy reassuringly. "I'm sure you're doing a great job. Just let me know if I can help you with anything."

Amy grinned. "I will. Thanks for the offer."

"I wouldn't go around making too many offers to work on the sixth-grade newspaper if I were you, Ms. Seventh-Grader," Maria teased. "Pretty soon you'll have your hands full with the *7&8 Gazette.*"

Elizabeth felt her heart lift a little. "Yeah, I guess you're right. I'm actually planning to go talk to them tomorrow. I'm pretty nervous about it, to tell you the truth, but I'm also really excited."

"You should be," Amy said. "It's such an amazing opportunity for you."

"Yeah, it should be a challenge," Elizabeth said, smiling.

"Oh, hey, speaking of challenges, how was that party you went to on Friday night?"

Elizabeth sighed. She had purposely avoided mentioning the party. She just wanted to relax and enjoy her lunch with Amy and Maria. But she knew there wasn't much point in keeping secrets from her friends. "Actually, I had a terrible time," she admitted.

"Really?" Amy asked, sounding surprised.

Elizabeth nodded, making a face. "They played this totally stupid game called Spin the Bottle, and I was supposed to kiss Bruce Patman."

"You're kidding," Amy said, her eyes widening. "They made you kiss that obnoxious guy?"

"Well, that was the idea," Elizabeth said. "Only, it didn't exactly work out that way." Taking a deep breath, Elizabeth told the whole story—how she was trying so hard to fit in, how she didn't even realize what the bottle game was all about until it was too late, how everyone began to laugh at her.

"That's terrible," Maria said, shaking her head.

"What an awful experience for you to go through."

"Those people can be so mean," Amy agreed. "I think you should just forget about them. You don't need friends like that."

"I don't know, you guys. I'm sure they can be really nice some—"

Elizabeth broke off as she saw Janet and Kimberly walking toward her table. Her heart sank as she realized what they wanted. She'd managed to forget about her dare, but now there was no turning away.

"Hey, Elizabeth," Janet said, "I've come up with your dare."

"What dare?" Amy asked.

Elizabeth squirmed uncomfortably in her seat. She had a pretty good idea what Amy would have to say about Elizabeth doing a dare.

"Elizabeth? What dare?" Amy repeated.

"Elizabeth had to leave Tom's party right before her turn in Truth or Dare," Janet explained. "So I was in charge of coming up with a dare for her to do this week."

Kimberly giggled. "And it's really a good one—nice and juicy."

"What is it?" Elizabeth asked quietly, even though she really didn't want to know the answer.

"Well, you're going to do it on Friday, here in the cafeteria," Janet started, then paused for effect.

"Yeah?" Elizabeth prompted, curious despite herself.

Janet smiled at her brightly. "You're going to walk over to Bruce Patman's table and give him a kiss on the lips in front of the entire school. Toodles!"

Elizabeth watched in a daze as Janet and Kimberly walked away. She felt as though someone had punched her in the stomach. The idea of kissing Bruce Patman was horrible. The idea of kissing him in front of the entire school was too awful for words.

She looked at her friends, unable to speak.

"You're *not* doing that," Amy insisted. "That's the most ridiculous thing I've ever heard of in my life. I mean, what's the point?"

"I agree," Maria said firmly. "It's moronic, and if they think you'd actually go through with something like that, they're crazy."

Elizabeth knew that her friends were right, but she also knew that there was no easy way out. She was determined to make it as a seventh-grader no matter what, and if that meant she'd have to do things that she thought were silly, then that's what she would do. She couldn't let down her parents, her teachers, or herself.

"I know it seems stupid and everything, but I have to go through with it," Elizabeth told her friends. "I just don't have a choice."

"Of course you have a choice," Amy protested. "You don't have to do stupid stuff like that just to be accepted. That's not like you, and you know it."

"It's different in the seventh grade," Elizabeth said, knowing that what she was saying sounded weak. "The pressures to be like everyone else are really strong."

"Why do you want to be like everyone else?" Maria asked. "You're great the way you are."

Why can't they just let this go? Elizabeth thought miserably. *I just want to do it and get it over with and not think about it too much.*

"I really appreciate what you guys are saying, but this is just something I have to do," Elizabeth said, wiping her hands and throwing her napkin on her tray. "And I actually have to go now and look over my notes for a quiz I have in my next class."

Elizabeth stood up quickly and walked away from the table. *Why does seventh grade have to be so hard?* she wondered.

"These look really interesting," Jed Michaels, the editor-in-chief of the *7&8 Gazette*, told Elizabeth on Tuesday afternoon. Elizabeth was sitting with him in the newspaper office while he looked over some of the articles she had written for the *Sixers* that year. "You're obviously a great journalist and editor."

Elizabeth leaned forward eagerly. "Thanks," she said, trying to contain her enthusiasm. Jed was in the eighth grade, and Elizabeth had always looked up to him. He had curly, sandy-colored hair and wore gold glasses with round frames. More important, he was a great editor, and she couldn't believe she'd actually have the chance to work with him.

She glanced at the important-looking desk right next to his. It was covered with papers and books. She felt a slight tingle as she imagined herself sitting there.

"Did I mention that I actually helped start the *Sixers*?" Elizabeth asked.

Jed looked up from the pile of articles in front of

him. "Yes, you've mentioned that twice already," he replied with a straight face.

"Oh, sorry," Elizabeth mumbled nervously. "Well, I just want you to know that I'm a really hard worker. I understand if you don't have any editorial positions open right now, but I'd love to write a column for the *7&8 Gazette*. I have some really good ideas for new columns."

Jed took his glasses off and held them in his right hand. He didn't say anything for what seemed like a long time. Did he expect her to start telling him her ideas? Or did he think she was being too aggressive?

"We do have a place for you at the paper," he finally said.

"You do?" Elizabeth practically jumped out of her seat. "That's great! I'm a really fast writer and I can start right away!"

"Actually, the job I have in mind for you isn't as a writer."

Elizabeth's heart beat from excitement. *He's about to make me an editor! This is turning out even better than I'd ever imagined!*

"We need someone to help us out around the office," Jed explained. "You know, making photocopies and organizing—that sort of thing. We're short of hands."

Elizabeth felt her whole body deflate. "Photocopies?" she repeated.

"Yes," Jed confirmed, looking at her steadily. "Although actually there *is* something else."

"There is?" Elizabeth asked hopefully.

"We also could use you to deliver some of the papers to different locations around the school. If you want to start right now, that would be great."

Delivering? I'm an editor-in-chief! Elizabeth was biting her lip. She didn't want to be rude or ungrateful, but it didn't seem fair. She took a deep breath and looked around the cluttered office. *It could be fun to work here,* she thought resignedly. *And maybe if I get my foot in the door, I'll eventually get to write some articles.*

"OK," Elizabeth said. "I'll take it."

"That's great," Jed said, smiling for the first time. "Here's a stack of our recent issue. Can you leave fifty copies in the lunchroom, twenty copies in the teachers' lounge, and one hundred copies in the lobby of the gym?"

"Sure thing," Elizabeth said, getting to her feet and taking the stack of papers. *It's not exactly what I'd imagined, but it's a start,* she told herself as she left the office, swallowing her pride.

I thought journalism was supposed to be glamorous and exciting, Jessica thought on Tuesday afternoon. She was sitting at a table in the *Sixers* office as the staff talked about the same dumb article for what seemed like an hour.

"Jessica, I don't see your article here," Amy said as she rifled through some papers on the table. "Did you give it to me? Maybe I misplaced it."

"Oh, I'm so stupid," Jessica said, hitting her forehead with her hand. "I left it at home. Would it be okay if I brought it to you tomorrow?"

That is, I'll bring to you tomorrow if I can actually get around to writing that boring thing.

"The paper starts printing at seven thirty tomorrow morning," Amy said. "Could you bring it by my house tonight?"

"Uh . . . well, how about if I bring it here tomorrow morning before seven thirty?" Jessica asked. "I just want to polish it up a little bit tonight."

"Hmm," Amy said thoughtfully. "Well, I guess that would be all right. Just make sure you bring it on time. Otherwise, it won't make it into this week's issue."

"No problem," Jessica said. She'd worry about writing the article later. Maybe she'd get some brilliant idea or something that night.

"OK, everyone, that's it for today," Amy announced.

Finally, Jessica thought, shutting her notebook. As she jumped out of her seat, she spotted Elizabeth in the doorway. The twins were planning on walking home from school together.

Jessica immediately turned to Todd. He was sitting in on *Sixers* meetings that week, since he'd be editing some sports articles for the upcoming issue.

"That's a great shirt you're wearing, Todd," she gushed. "It looks fabulous on you."

Todd glanced down at his shirt in confusion. "Uh, thanks. It's just a plain white T-shirt. I've had it forever."

Jessica laughed loudly. "You're so modest. Oh, look, there's Elizabeth. I'm surprised she has time to come by here. I mean, between all her work and her new social life and everything."

"What do you mean by her new social life?" Todd asked, frowning.

"You know," Jessica said. "Like all the parties she's been going to and all the new friends she's been making."

"Hey, guys!" Elizabeth said to Jessica and Todd as they walked through the door. "So how does it feel to be guest-editing, Todd?"

"Fine," Todd said curtly. "Excuse me, I have a lot to do."

Todd quickly walked away.

Elizabeth looked after him with a frown. "What's wrong with him?"

"I guess he's upset about the kiss," Jessica replied.

"The kiss?" Elizabeth repeated as they walked down the hallway together.

"The kiss you have to give Bruce on Friday."

"How does he know about it?" Elizabeth asked. She turned to face Jessica. "And how do you know about it?"

Jessica laughed. "Are you kidding? Everybody knows about it. It's all anyone's talking about."

Elizabeth widened her eyes in horror. "What are they saying?"

"Hmm, let's see," Jessica said thoughtfully. "I'm trying to remember what exactly I heard. Oh, yeah—they're just saying that this will be your chance to prove you're not a baby after all," Jessica lied.

"A baby? Why would they say that?"

"I guess people thought it was pretty weird that you didn't kiss Bruce at the party," Jessica explained lightly.

Elizabeth felt her face get hot. "*You* know about that?" she asked, embarrassed at having been caught in a lie.

"Please, Elizabeth," Jessica said, rolling her eyes. "The whole school knows about it."

"Oh, great," Elizabeth groaned. "That's all I need."

"Anyway," Jessica continued. "When you didn't kiss him at the party, everyone kind of thought you were too much of a baby to be in seventh grade."

"They did?" Elizabeth asked miserably. That was exactly what she'd been afraid of.

"Yep," Jessica confirmed. "But now's your chance to prove that you're really not a total wimp. All you have to do is kiss Bruce Patman in front of the whole school, and everyone will know you're up to being in seventh grade."

"Right," Elizabeth mumbled.

"Well, I'll see you later, Lizzie," Jessica said as they walked down the front steps of the school.

"What? I thought we were walking home together," Elizabeth said, surprised.

"I just remembered, I can't. I have to get together with Todd and Amy about the camping trip," Jessica lied.

"But you just saw them," Elizabeth protested.

"*That* was about the *Sixers*, Lizzie. *This* is about the camping trip." *And about pushing you just a little closer to the edge*, she added to herself as she walked around a corner, leaving her sister behind her.

Ten

Yuck, Jessica thought on Tuesday night as she read over the first sentence of her *Sixers* article. For about the fiftieth time that night, she crumpled the paper she was writing on into a ball and threw it into the overflowing trash can by her desk.

It was ten o'clock, and Jessica just didn't see how she'd ever be able to finish the article before it was due the next morning. She didn't have a single interesting thing to say about the sixth-grade camping trip.

Jessica put her head in her hands and groaned. Normally, she didn't get so worked up about assignments she couldn't complete. Whenever she was stuck on a homework assignment or a paper she had to write, she knew she could go to Elizabeth for help. But it was different now. She was supposed to be making Elizabeth jealous of her success on the *Sixers*—she couldn't let on that one sentence into her article she was already bored to tears.

Suddenly Jessica had an idea. *What if I somehow convince Elizabeth that the* Sixers *is falling apart without her? She wouldn't be able to stand it—she'd come running back to sixth grade just to save the newspaper!*

Jessica jumped up from her desk with her notebook in hand.

"Elizabeth! Could you come here?" she yelled out in the hallway. She ran back to her desk and leaned over her notebook with her head in her hands.

"What? What is it?" Elizabeth asked breathlessly as she ran through Jessica's door. "Are you sick? Is there a fire?"

"No, it's nothing like that, but it *is* pretty bad," Jessica said in her weariest and most troubled voice. "Maybe you should sit down."

Elizabeth sat down on the edge of Jessica's bed and crossed her arms in front of her. "OK, tell me what's wrong."

"Do you promise not to tell anyone what I'm about to tell you?" Jessica asked. "Especially Amy?"

Elizabeth nodded solemnly. "I promise."

Jessica drew in a deep breath. "It's about the Sixers," she began, then hesitated for dramatic effect.

"Yes?" Elizabeth prompted.

"Well, Amy's in a lot of trouble with this week's issue," Jessica continued in a confidential tone. "It's just too much responsibility for her, so she's assigned extra articles to me to help her meet the deadline."

"Really?" Elizabeth asked, her brow creased with worry. "I had no idea. Why didn't Amy tell me?"

"I guess she didn't want you to worry," Jessica replied.

"I feel terrible," Elizabeth said, shaking her head. "It's all my fault. I didn't stay around long enough to show her the routine. And I guess I've been so wrapped up in my schoolwork and everything that I haven't really been paying attention to how things are going for her."

"Yeah, well, there's something you can do to help straighten things out," Jessica told her.

"There is?" Elizabeth asked.

"Yeah. I'm supposed to write two articles tonight and there's no way I can do both," Jessica said. "I was wondering if you could write one of them."

"No problem," Elizabeth said instantly. "What's the article about?"

"You can write the one about the camping trip," Jessica replied, handing her sister her notebook. "Here are all the notes I've taken."

Elizabeth flipped through the pages. "This should be pretty easy. I can have this finished in about an hour."

"You're the greatest," Jessica said. "Oh, but maybe we shouldn't tell Amy that you wrote it."

"That's a good idea," Elizabeth said. "I don't want to embarrass her or anything. I'll just give the article to you so you can hand it in, and Amy will think you wrote it."

"Perfect," Jessica said.

"Hi, Elizabeth. I've got some great lip gloss you can borrow on Friday," Leslie said as she walked by

Elizabeth's locker on Wednesday morning. "I'm sure Bruce will love it."

Elizabeth turned around to see Leslie, Helen, and Kerry laughing as they continued walking down the hall. She felt a chill up and down her spine, and she wanted to jump inside her locker and spend the rest of the day there.

Just ignore those girls, Elizabeth told herself. *They're not your real friends.*

As she continued taking her books out of her backpack, she heard a group of guys laughing behind her.

"Pucker up, Wakefield," Rick Hunter said, pursing his lips together and making a slurping sound.

"Bruce! Bruce! Kiss me! Kiss me!" Tom McKay said as he clasped his hands to his chest.

Elizabeth slammed her locker door and spun around. "Excuse me," she said sternly as she pushed by them and walked quickly down the hall.

I'm the joke of the school, she thought, her pulse racing. The dreaded kiss was supposed to happen the day after next. *How did I get myself into this? I wish Friday would never come!*

"Hey, thanks for doing that article," Jessica said on Wednesday night. She was sprawled out on her bed, and Elizabeth had just come into her room. "It was really great, and Amy loved it."

"I'm glad I could help," Elizabeth said, smiling.

"It's too bad you can't still be on the *Sixers*," Jessica continued. "I mean, I know you love being in seventh grade and everything, but it's sad to see something you worked so hard for going down the tubes like that."

Elizabeth let out a heavy sigh. It *had* felt great to write that article the night before. Writing it made Elizabeth realize how much she missed working on the *Sixers*. After school that day she'd spent two hours photocopying in the *7&8 Gazette*'s office— hardly a fun assignment. All she could think about was how much responsibility she'd had as the *Sixers* editor-in-chief.

Jessica sat up and began sorting through a pile of sweaters and jeans. "I have so much to pack for the camping trip this weekend. Good thing I bought this huge backpack."

"It sounds like it's going to be a lot of fun," Elizabeth said, looking longingly at Jessica's camping gear. There was nothing she'd rather do than go on that camping trip with her friends. She'd been feeling so far away from the people who were the closest to her, and a camping trip would be the perfect way to reconnect. "I read all your notes about the activities that are planned for it. I wish I could go."

"Oh, well, I'm sure you'll be invited to another great party this weekend," Jessica said. "You had such a great time at last week's party and everything."

"Right," Elizabeth mumbled.

As Jessica began packing and humming to herself, Elizabeth felt even worse. She knew she should be happy that Jessica was so excited about the trip. After all, her own life as a seventh-grader was starting to come together—academically, anyway. She'd done well on a science quiz that morning, and she was loving the books she was reading for her history and English classes. All her teachers seemed really pleased with her work.

But somehow her academic success wasn't really making her happy—not happy enough. She missed working on the *Sixers* and spending time with her friends, she was miserable she couldn't go on the camping trip, she wasn't feeling close to Jessica, and—worst of all—she was dreading having to kiss Bruce in front of the entire school on Friday. All in all, seventh grade was turning out to be pretty terrible.

Suddenly, everything seemed to be pointing in one direction: she had to quit seventh grade.

"Hi, honey, what's up?" Mr. Wakefield asked when Elizabeth walked through the door of his study on Wednesday night.

Elizabeth was having a hard time breathing. She'd decided to tell her parents separately about her decision to go back to sixth grade. She didn't think she could handle telling them both at the same time.

"Dad, there's something I need to talk to you about," Elizabeth said, her voice shaking.

"I'm glad you're here," Mr. Wakefield said. "Have a seat. I want to talk to you about something, too."

"Sure," Elizabeth said, sitting down. "What's up?"

"Your mother and I have been talking about your being in the seventh grade," Mr. Wakefield said.

"Yes?" Elizabeth prodded.

"And I know we've said it before, but I want you

to know just how proud of you we are, sweetheart," he said, smiling.

"Mmm," Elizabeth mumbled.

Mr. Wakefield beamed. "You've really been working hard, and Mr. Bowman called today to let us know that all your teachers are raving about you."

"They are?" Elizabeth asked, pleased and disappointed at the same time.

"Apparently, you've handled the challenge beautifully," Mr. Wakefield said. "You really seem happy about your decision, and that makes us happy, too."

Elizabeth smiled weakly. Her parents' praise was even more important to her than her teachers'. There was no way she could disappoint her father. She could handle missing the camping trip. She could even handle kissing Bruce Patman. "I am happy," she confirmed. "And I think I did make the right decision."

Elizabeth stood up to leave.

"What did you want to talk to me about?" Mr. Wakefield asked as she opened the door.

"Oh, I just wanted to tell you how great everything was going," Elizabeth said, swallowing the lump that was forming in her throat. "Good night."

"You can go blind if you read too much, you know," Jessica said as she breezed into the family room on Thursday afternoon. Elizabeth was spread out on the couch, reading a play for English class. It was called *Of Mice and Men*, by John Steinbeck, and Elizabeth loved it. She was so happy when she was doing her work, she wished that was all she had to worry about.

"I don't think that's been medically proven," Elizabeth said, not looking up from her book.

"Yeah, well, every time I've seen you recently, you've had a book in front of your face," Jessica said. "I know you like to study, but this is getting ridiculous."

Elizabeth pried her eyes away from her book. "Where have you been?" she asked, resigning herself to the fact that her peace and quiet were momentarily over.

"I just had the biggest banana split of my life at Casey's," Jessica said, rubbing her tummy. "I honestly think I could eat three banana splits a day and not need any other food."

"Sounds yummy," Elizabeth said. She picked her book back up, hoping that Jessica would take the hint that she wanted to go back to her reading.

"You were certainly the flavor of the day," Jessica said, ignoring Elizabeth's hint.

"Why's that?" Elizabeth asked. She was sure she didn't want to know the answer.

"All anyone was talking about was the kiss you have to give Bruce tomorrow," Jessica said.

Elizabeth glanced at her sister. "Like, what kind of stuff were they saying?" she asked fearfully.

"Well, that group of girls—Leslie, Kerry, and Helen—were saying that they knew there was no way you'd ever go through with it," Jessica said. "Leslie said that what happened at Tom's party was obvious proof that you just weren't up for it."

Elizabeth rolled her eyes. "That girl really gets on my nerves. Anything else?"

"Well, the Unicorns are taking bets on it," Jessica said casually. "Everyone except me, of course. If Lila's right, she'll win a bundle."

Elizabeth bit her lip. It was bad enough that people were gossiping about her dare—now Jessica's snobby friends were treating it like it was some kind of sporting event. "And what exactly did Lila bet?" she asked stiffly.

"She's the only one who bet that you would kiss Bruce tomorrow," Jessica said. "At least if you don't go through with it, nobody will be surprised. In fact, I don't think anyone's really expecting you to do it."

Elizabeth felt her face flush with anger. Even though the thought of kissing Bruce in front of the school—or anywhere, for that matter—was totally disgusting to her, part of her felt an intense need to prove to everyone that they were wrong.

"Well, I think there will be a lot of shocked faces tomorrow," Elizabeth said, narrowing her eyes.

"Hmm," Jessica mumbled distractedly. "Oh, hey, did I mention that Todd was getting really miffed?"

"No, you didn't," Elizabeth said, annoyed.

"Some seventh- and eighth-grade guys came by the booth we were sitting at and started teasing him," Jessica explained.

Elizabeth slammed her book shut. "What did they say to him?"

Jessica reached for the remote control on the coffee table and flipped on one of her favorite soap operas. She sat down on the other end of the couch and crossed her arms behind her head. "Oh, just something about how he was off your dance card and Bruce had replaced him. Stuff like that. Todd caused a real commotion."

Elizabeth stared at Jessica in shock. "What do you mean?"

"He almost got in a fight with a guy," Jessica said. "Some jerk came up to him and said something about how you had gotten tired of little boys like Todd and were ready to move on to real men."

Elizabeth stood up from the couch and threw her book on the floor. "That's the most obnoxious thing I've ever heard. Those guys think they're so tough just because they're in the seventh and eighth grade—they think they can get away with anything." She buried her face in her hands and groaned. "After Friday, Todd probably won't want to talk to me again, and I wouldn't blame him."

"Does this mean you're still going through with it?" Jessica asked without moving her gaze from the television set.

"I'm still going through with it," Elizabeth muttered bitterly. She wasn't about to look wimpy in front of those seventh-grade bullies.

"Hey, Jessica," Steven said as he poked his head into Jessica's room on Thursday night, "you got a minute?"

"It depends," Jessica said, looking away from the mirror on her dressing table. She was in the middle of her usual nighttime routine, which included brushing her hair one hundred times. "What's up?"

Steven walked in and shut the door. "It's about

Elizabeth," he said with a serious tone.

"What about her?" Jessica asked.

"I've been thinking about that stupid dare she's supposed to do tomorrow, and I think it's a really bad idea," Steven said.

"I wouldn't worry if I were you," Jessica said nonchalantly, looking back at her reflection in the mirror.

"Listen, Jessica, this whole thing is over the top," he said, moving closer to her dressing table. "I mean, enough's enough. She shouldn't be kissing *anyone* in the middle of the cafeteria, let alone that idiot Bruce Patman."

"It's sweet that you're so concerned," Jessica said sarcastically.

"I mean it," Steven said sternly. "How far does she have to go before she realizes that she shouldn't be a seventh-grader? I think we should tell her not to go through with it."

Jessica put down her brush and faced her brother. "Steven, Steven, Steven. I thought you were supposed to be the expert on psychology."

Steven winced. "I am, but what's that got to do with it?"

Jessica sighed impatiently. "Then you should know that the way to get Elizabeth *not* to do something is to totally build it up and tease her like it's this great, funny event. If we act scared, she'll just get brave and go through with it, but—"

"But if we tease her," Steven broke in, "she'll just get nervous and—"

"—and chicken out!" Jessica finished.

Eleven

The cafeteria was full of laughter and whispers. Elizabeth sat alone at a long table. Everyone was staring at her and pointing.

"She'll never do it," Janet Howell said.

"She belongs back in kindergarten," Leslie said.

"What a loser," Rick Hunter said.

Elizabeth stood up and walked toward the table where Bruce Patman was sitting. Everyone stood up, forming two long rows leading to Bruce's table. As she walked between the rows of onlookers, Elizabeth saw Amy and Todd looking at her in horror.

"You don't have to do this," Amy cautioned.

"If you do it, I won't be your boyfriend anymore," Todd said ominously.

She walked farther and saw Jessica in the line. "You have to do it," Jessica told her. "It's the only way to prove you belong in the seventh grade."

All the teachers looked at her as she passed by. "What's

she doing?" Mr. Bowman asked.

"She's too smart to go along with peer pressure," Mrs. Arnette said.

Finally, Elizabeth reached Bruce, who was grinning at her in a disgusting way.

"I've been waiting for this," Bruce said. "I hope you get it right this time and don't chicken out like before."

Elizabeth closed her eyes and heard the chanting that filled the room. "Kiss him! Kiss him! Kiss him! Kiss him!"

The alarm went off on Elizabeth's clock, and she opened her eyes. *It was just a dream*, she realized. She put her hand on her forehead. She was breaking out in a cold sweat.

Today's the day, she thought gloomily. She reached down and pulled the covers over her head, wishing that she could stay hidden like that until the day was over.

I could call in sick, she thought. *But nobody would buy that—they'd just think I was chickening out like before.*

Her whole body felt stiff and tight. There was no way out. *I have to do it, I have to do, I have to do it.* If she didn't go through with the dare, nobody in the seventh grade would talk to her—they wouldn't want to be associated with such a baby. It would be awful to stay in seventh grade with that hanging over her every day. And she had to stay in seventh grade. She was loving all her classes, and most important, her parents were counting on her. They'd be heartbroken if she failed to live up to this challenge.

She sat up and shook the covers off. *It'll be over before I know it*, she assured herself. *How bad can it be?*

* * *

"Elizabeth, don't you think you'd like to wear something else today?" Jessica asked at the breakfast table on Friday morning as she examined Elizabeth's blue jeans and light-blue oxford shirt. Mr. and Mrs. Wakefield had to leave for work early that day, so the kids were eating alone. "I mean all the attention *is* going to be on you."

"I like the way I look," Elizabeth snapped. "And I don't care what anybody else thinks."

"Touchy, touchy, touchy," Jessica said, shaking her head. "Somebody woke up on the wrong side of the bed today."

Jessica could barely contain her grin as she saw how petrified her sister looked. *Her face is as white as the milk in her cereal, and she's barely taken a bite of anything. There's no way she's going to go through with the kiss today.*

"You might want to use some Chap Stick," Steven suggested. "Your lips are looking pretty chapped."

"My lips are fine," Elizabeth said without looking up from her cereal. "And besides, what do you care about my chapped lips?"

"I just thought since you were going to be kissing Bruce today, you might want them to be in better condition," Steven said.

"Can we please talk about something else?" Elizabeth asked curtly. "I feel like I'm going to throw up."

"Better to throw up now than in the cafeteria," Jessica said. "Can you imagine throwing up in front of the whole school like that? That would really do wonders for your reputation."

Jessica watched as Elizabeth's face turned paler. She knew she was being a little mean, but it was for Elizabeth's own good. The more afraid she made her feel about the kiss, the less chance there was of her going through with it.

"I already asked if we could please not talk about it," Elizabeth said, putting her hands over her ears.

"I don't think you should be so upset about it," Jessica said. "It's just a kiss, and in the long run it will be worth it. It wouldn't be the worst thing if Todd broke up with you, anyway."

"Broke up with me?" Elizabeth asked, taking her hands off her ears. "Did he say something to you?"

"Well, not exactly. All I'm saying is that it would be totally humiliating for him to see his girlfriend kiss another guy in front of the whole school," Jessica said matter-of-factly.

"You're probably right about that, Jessica," Steven agreed. He turned to Elizabeth. "You really couldn't blame him if he did break up with you."

Elizabeth's upper lip began to quiver.

"Besides, you're in the seventh grade," Jessica said. "You can't really have a sixth-grade boyfriend. I mean, he's a nice guy and all, but he's not what you need if you want to really fit in with the other people in your class."

"Excuse me," Elizabeth said, standing up from the table. "I have to go now." She picked up her backpack and walked outside through the kitchen door.

"It looks like your plan, thanks to me, is working," Steven said, patting himself on the back once Elizabeth was gone.

Jessica folded her arms. "I think it is—thanks to me!"

*   *   *

Elizabeth walked into homeroom as quietly as possible, aware that clusters of students were looking at her and giggling. *Don't think about it, don't think about it, don't think about it,* she told herself as she found a seat as far away from the other students as possible.

As she sat down, she thought about her old sixth-grade homeroom. She had sat with Jessica and Amy. Everyone had been friendly and happy to see her, and it had been a great way to start the morning. Now she hated homeroom. It was easier when a class was going on and the teacher was talking—then she didn't feel any pressure to socialize.

She had grabbed the latest issue of the *Sixers* from the bench outside homeroom, but she hesitated before opening it. She didn't know if, on top of everything else, she could bear to see a disastrous issue of the *Sixers*. But she also didn't want to just sit there and listen to the class whisper about her. Her heart thumping, she slowly opened the paper.

When she saw the layout, she gasped. Amy had obviously done some experimenting—but instead of looking terrible, the paper had a fresh, eye-catching design. As Elizabeth began to read, she found that the articles were intesting and well written. *What was Jessica talking about?* Elizabeth wondered. *The* Sixers *looks better than ever. Amy obviously hasn't had any problems at all.*

She was happy that her friend had done such a good job, but she couldn't help feeling a little sad at the same time. Apparently, everything was going along fine without her. She had loved feeling needed the other night when Jessica asked her to write that article, but obviously, they didn't need her at all. And they certainly didn't need her at the *7&8 Gazette*. She'd suggested five different article topics to Jed the day before, and he had just dismissed all of them. He said she'd have to wait a few more months before she could really start doing any writing.

Elizabeth looked up as Leslie, Helen, and Kerry started filing into homeroom. They were all wearing hip, cool outfits—the kind of stuff Jessica would probably think was really sophisticated. Helen had on bell-bottoms and a long, ribbed T-shirt, and Leslie and Kerry both wore miniskirts and tiny sweaters. Elizabeth looked down at her oxford shirt and jeans and suddenly wished she were wearing something else. *I should have listened to Jessica,* she thought. *I do look pretty boring and juvenile like this.*

"I wonder what's for lunch today," Leslie said, taking a seat next to Helen and Kerry in the row behind Elizabeth. "Do you think they're going to give out Hershey's Kisses?"

"I heard they were serving a new casserole called Tuna Kiss," Helen joked.

Elizabeth wanted to slide down in her seat as the giggles grew louder. *Doesn't anyone have anything better to talk about?* she wondered, both embarrassed and exasperated.

But she knew that the girls' teasing was really the least of her problems. And as much as she hated homeroom, she was filled with dread as the bell for first period rang. The moment when she'd have to kiss Bruce was getting closer and closer. *I wish I could stop time,* she thought as she got up to go to her first class.

Twelve

"Elizabeth, you haven't taken one bite of your sandwich, and you look like you're about to be sick," Amy said to Elizabeth at lunch on Friday. "I know I've said it before, but you really don't have to do this."

"She's right," Maria agreed. "It isn't worth putting yourself through this torture."

Elizabeth looked down at her lunch tray. In a way, she felt safe with her friends, as if somehow they could keep the inevitable from happening. But she knew that they really couldn't—and that if she opened her mouth to speak or eat, she'd just choke on tears.

"We're your friends and we care about you," Maria went on. "You don't have to worry about those other jerks. You're too good for them, anyway."

Elizabeth knew that her friends were right, but that didn't help. "I have to do this," she told them, wiping away the tears that were forming in the corners of her eyes. "I want to stay in seventh grade. My parents would be crushed if I couldn't stick it out."

"But I still don't understand what kissing Bruce Patman, the biggest creep in the whole school, has to do with staying in seventh grade," Amy protested.

Elizabeth sighed heavily. It had all seemed so clear a little while ago, but now she was having a hard time understanding it herself.

For the one hundredth time, she went over the list of reasons why she had to kiss Bruce. If she didn't do it, she wouldn't have any seventh-grade friends, and people would think she was immature. Everyone, including Jessica, would be able to say that they were right—she just wasn't socially sophisticated enough to be in the seventh grade. Also, if she didn't do it, they'd probably think of something worse that she had to do—although it was hard to imagine anything worse than kissing Bruce Patman on the lips in front of the whole world.

Before Elizabeth could say anything to her friends, Janet and Kimberly came over to her table. Elizabeth felt a cold sweat on her back, and she remembered the nightmare she'd had that morning.

"OK, it's time," Janet said. "Are you ready?"

"Actually, I just wanted to finish my sandwich," Elizabeth whispered. She picked up her sandwich and took a bite, forcing herself to swallow.

"Look, we don't have all day," Janet said nastily. "Lunch period will be over soon. Everybody's waiting."

"Don't do it," Amy said under her breath. "It's not too late to change your mind."

"Your friend is right," Janet said, even though Elizabeth knew she was fully aware of what Amy's name was. "You don't have to do it. If you can live with being called the baby of seventh grade, nobody else cares. I mean, it's not as if anyone thinks you're really going through with it."

"That's right," Kimberly said. "Everyone's sure you're not up to it. I even bet five dollars that you wouldn't do it."

Elizabeth's pulse raced with anger. She stood up and looked from Janet to Kimberly. "Well, you're going to be out five dollars," she informed her.

Elizabeth realized that the cafeteria had fallen silent and that everyone was looking in her direction. Even the teachers seemed to sense that she was about to do something. Mr. Bowman was looking at her with a bewildered expression.

All my teachers are so proud of me, Elizabeth thought despairingly. In a few minutes, their opinion of her would change forever.

She looked over at the Unicorner, the club's lunchroom table. Jessica mouthed the words "Go for it" from across the room. Then she looked at Todd, who was sitting with Winston at the table next to hers. He wouldn't even look at her. He was staring down at the table, as if seeing her would be too painful.

Elizabeth took one step toward Bruce's table. He was sitting with his friends, and he looked exactly as he had in her nightmare that morning—he wore that same disgusting expression. *What a gross creep,* she thought.

She took two more steps. She imagined her parents'

faces the first night they told her that her teachers wanted her to be in the seventh grade. *We're so proud of you*, she could hear them say. *You've really worked hard, and it's all paid off. You've made us so happy.*

I can't let them down, she told herself for the millionth time. She walked closer and closer to Bruce's table until she was standing right in front of him.

She could hear Jessica's words about how everyone thought she was a baby. She kept seeing the stupid smile on Kimberly's face when she said she'd bet five dollars that Elizabeth wouldn't go through with it. She remembered the sting she'd felt when someone at the party had said she belonged in the fourth grade.

She could almost hear people breathing, it was so quiet.

"She's going to do it," somebody shrieked.

"It's Patman's lucky day," another voice said.

Elizabeth leaned across the table until her face was three inches from Bruce's. His eyes were closed, and his lips were puckered up.

She drew in a deep breath and looked around the room. Every single person in the room was waiting. *This is it*, she told herself.

She moved an inch closer until she could feel Bruce's breath on her face. Then she froze.

What are you doing? she suddenly thought in a panic. *This isn't like you at all. You're acting like somebody else—like somebody who cares a ton what other people think.*

Elizabeth sprang back from the table. "I can't do it," she announced, and she strode across the cafeteria.

*   *   *

Elizabeth held her head high as the cafeteria grew loud with frenzied talking and laughing.

"Way to go, Elizabeth," Amy said as Elizabeth sat back down at her table. Amy threw her arms around her friend. "I knew you couldn't go through with it."

"You really showed those jerks," Maria added. "Bruce's ego will be ruined forever now."

"You guys are the greatest," Elizabeth said, biting into her tuna sandwich. "I should have listened to you from the start. I don't need friends like that. You guys are all I need."

"Hey, how about me?" Todd asked as he appeared from behind. "Don't you need me, too?"

Elizabeth stood up and gave Todd a big hug. "You bet I do," she said. "I've missed you like crazy."

"Me, too," Todd said, taking a seat.

"I knew you were just a kid," Janet Howell said, approaching the table.

Elizabeth gave Janet a big smile. "You're right. I am a kid. And I'm happy to be one."

"Elizabeth!" Jessica exclaimed breathlessly as she ran up to the table. "You didn't do it! I *knew* you wouldn't be able to stay away from sixth grade for long."

Elizabeth looked lovingly at Jessica. "I'm still going to be in the seventh grade. I'm just through trying to be something that I'm not. And if that means nobody's going to talk to me—well, then, there's nothing I can do about it."

"But—" Jessica began, then fell silent, looking completely dejected.

"We'll still be able to hang out, Jess, I promise," Elizabeth said to comfort her. "In fact, we *better* be able to hang out, especially now that I won't have any friends in my grade."

"Well, as I said before, you're too good for those people anyway," Amy comforted. "It's their loss."

Elizabeth looked at Jessica and her friends and was filled with a deep sense of longing. She knew she had to stick it out in seventh grade—her parents and her teachers were counting on her—but now more than ever she wished she could go back to sixth grade. Her friends were all so accepting of her just the way she was. She'd never completely appreciated it until that moment. It was going to be a lonely year without any seventh-grade friends.

"Well, I guess you're not seventh-grade material after all," Leslie said as she walked by. "Too bad. I thought you had a lot of potential."

"I guess I'm just not as cool as you are, Leslie," Elizabeth said sarcastically. "And I'll just have to live with that."

"I'm so psyched to eat s'mores," Maria said on Friday afternoon in the school parking lot. "They're my favorite dessert." She turned to Elizabeth, who was waiting with her friends as they got ready to leave for the weekend. "Maybe we could bring you one."

Elizabeth laughed. "I don't think they'd last too well on the bus."

"I really wish you were coming with us," Amy said. "It won't be the same without you."

"Thanks," Elizabeth said sadly. "I wish I were coming, too."

"You could still change your mind and forget about being in the seventh grade," Jessica suggested hopefully.

Elizabeth smiled and looked at the ground. On the one hand, she'd love to forget about being in seventh grade. She really wanted to eat s'mores and hang out with her friends and with Jessica and work on the *Sixers* again. But her parents and her teachers were so pleased with her, and they expected her to stick with her decision.

"OK, everyone," Mr. Bowman announced from where the bus was parked nearby, "all aboard!"

"Have fun," Elizabeth said, forcing herself to smile as Jessica and her friends picked up their backpacks before climbing onto the bus.

Thirteen

"Hi, honey," Mrs. Wakefield said when Elizabeth walked through the kitchen door on Friday afternoon. "You don't look so happy. Is something wrong?"

"I'm OK," Elizabeth muttered, managing a smile. "I guess I'll go upstairs and do some homework."

"Actually, would you mind coming with me to run an errand?" Mrs. Wakefield asked. "I could really use your help."

"OK," Elizabeth said. Maybe helping her mother was just what she needed to take her mind off the long, lonely weekend ahead of her.

She followed her mother to the car and sat in the front seat. As her mother drove, Elizabeth looked out the window at the passing houses and yards and thought about what Jessica and her friends were doing at that moment. They were probably setting up their tents and planning their activities for the weekend. That night there'd probably be a cookout around the campfire with singing and s'mores. She felt an empty pit in her stomach, and she hoped her mother didn't notice the tears running down her cheeks.

It occurred to Elizabeth that they'd been driving for a really long time. What kind of errand were they running? She'd assumed they were just going to the mall, but it seemed as if they'd been in the car for an hour.

"Where are we going?" she asked finally.

"You'll see when we get there," Mrs. Wakefield said, smiling.

Soon they were surrounded by trees, and there wasn't a store in sight. Her mother pulled the car into a parking lot and drove up to where a crowd was gathered around a bunch of picnic tables.

It's my class! Elizabeth realized, so shocked it took her a few moments to find her voice. She turned to her mother. "What's going on, Mom?" she asked, her heart racing.

Mrs. Wakefield looked at her and smiled. "Welcome back to the sixth grade!"

Elizabeth leaped out of the car and went running up to Amy, Jessica, Maria, and Todd. "I can't believe it! I'm so happy to see you guys!" she exclaimed.

Amy gave her a huge hug. "Not as happy as we are to see you!"

"Especially me!" Jessica shouted, hugging Elizabeth from behind.

Mr. Bowman, Mrs. Arnette, and Mrs. Wakefield joined Elizabeth and her friends.

Elizabeth felt a twinge of worry. "Did I mess up in

my classes or something?" Elizabeth asked Mr. Bowman. "I was really trying hard to keep up with my work and everything."

"We know you were," Mr. Bowman assured her. "And we think you've been doing a wonderful job. All your teachers have been very pleased with your work."

Elizabeth frowned in confusion. "Then why am I being sent back to sixth grade? I mean, I'm totally ecstatic to be back, but I don't get it. Did I do something wrong?"

"You didn't do anything wrong," Mr. Bowman said, smiling at Mrs. Wakefield.

"Honey, this isn't a punishment," Mrs. Wakefield added as she put her arm around Elizabeth's shoulders.

Elizabeth looked around at her friends, teachers, and mother. "I'm still confused—I really thought I could handle it."

"You definitely can," Mr. Bowman said. "You've proved that you're obviously ready academically for the seventh grade."

"But just because you're ready academically," Mrs. Arnette chimed in, "doesn't mean you're ready socially."

Elizabeth blushed as she remembered that awful party and the pressure on her to kiss Bruce Patman earlier that day. "Well, *that's* the truth," she agreed. "But how did you all know that?"

"I overheard you talking to your friends this afternoon when we were getting ready to get on the bus. You were saying how much you wished you could go on the trip," Mr. Bowman explained.

"So Mr. Bowman called me and asked me what I thought about how you'd been doing lately," Mrs. Wakefield added. "I told him that I just assumed everything was going fine, but then the more I thought about it, the more I realized that I didn't really know. You've *said* that everything was fine, but I had to admit that you've seemed a bit preoccupied lately. I thought there might be something you weren't telling us."

"Yeah, I guess there was," Elizabeth admitted, looking at the ground.

"When I got off the phone with Mr. Bowman," Mrs. Wakefield continued, "I called your father, and we had a long talk about it. We both agreed that you just hadn't seemed like yourself lately."

"It's true," Elizabeth confessed. "I mean, I was really happy at first, and I loved my classes and everything, but I missed my friends. There was just too much social pressure being in the seventh grade, and I didn't feel like I could be myself."

"Oh, honey, I wish we'd known that," Mrs. Wakefield said, brushing aside a piece of Elizabeth's hair that had fallen from her ponytail. "Your father told me how you'd wanted to talk to him the other night about something, but before you got a chance, he started telling you how proud we were of you."

Elizabeth took a deep breath. "I was going to tell him that I wanted to go back to sixth grade, but he was so happy for me, I couldn't bear to let him down," she said softly.

Mrs. Wakefield grew misty-eyed. "We both feel

terrible that we made you feel like you had to do something you weren't ready for."

"And your other teachers and I feel bad, too," Mrs. Arnette added. "We didn't give enough thought to the difficult transition you might have socially."

Elizabeth smiled at her teachers and gave her mother a big hug. "Well, it's all worth it if I get to stay here for the weekend."

"Absolutely," Mrs. Arnette said. "After all, you're a sixth-grader."

"Welcome back, Lizzie," Jessica said. "I'm so glad things will be back to normal."

"That makes two of us," Elizabeth said, beaming.

"No, that makes three of us," Amy said.

"No, four!" Todd protested.

"Five!" Maria added.

As her friends all engulfed her in a hug, Elizabeth felt happier than she'd ever felt in her life.

"I'll have some more s'mores," Elizabeth joked that night. The class sat around the campfire, and Elizabeth was sitting between Amy and Todd. This time she was *glad* to be sitting around in a circle on a Friday night. In fact, she was so happy she didn't want the night to end.

"I'm so psyched you're back with us," Amy said. "I have to admit I was a little afraid of losing your friendship."

"That will never happen," Elizabeth said. "We're friends for life. You couldn't get rid of me if you tried."

"Well, the same goes for me," Amy said, roasting her marshmallow in the fire.

"Amy, there's something I wanted to talk to you about," Elizabeth said, taking on a more serious tone.

"Sure. What is it?" Amy asked.

"It's about the *Sixers*," Elizabeth started.

"Oh, well, you're definitely going to be editor-in-chief again," Amy said. "I just did it while you were gone, and like I said, it was a lot harder than I realized."

"Actually, I know you didn't have *that* much trouble," Elizabeth said, smiling.

Amy raised an eyebrow. "What are you talking about?"

"I saw a copy of this week's issue this morning, and it was one of the best issues I'd ever seen," Elizabeth explained. "You're a wonderful editor-in-chief."

Amy blushed. "Thanks. I have to admit, I did have a lot of fun with it. I guess I didn't want you to think I was eager to take over·your job or anything. After all, you *are* an awesome editor, and I was afraid you'd think I was competing with you."

Elizabeth grinned. "I think the *Sixers* is big enough for more than one awesome editor-in-chief, don't you?"

Amy's eyes lit up. "What exactly are you getting at?"

"Well," Elizabeth explained, "I was hoping that when we get back to school next week you would be my co-editor-in-chief."

"Are you kidding? I'd love to!" Amy exclaimed.

"Then let's roast some marshmallows and celebrate!" Elizabeth said gleefully.

*　　*　　*

"It's about time you've come back to the sixth grade," Jessica said to Elizabeth on Friday night. They decided to share a tent, just the two of them, to make up for the time they'd spent apart lately. "I missed you like crazy."

"Oh, yeah?" Elizabeth said, snuggling down into her sleeping bag. "You seemed to be doing all right without me around—in your career as a journalist and everything."

"Oh, that stuff. Actually I have a tiny confession to make." She paused, grinning sheepishly. "I was really only pretending that I was having such a blast so that you'd come back to sixth grade."

Elizabeth started laughing.

"What's so funny?" Jessica asked, frowning.

"I have to say, I kind of suspected something weird was going on. I mean, I *know* that you're not crazy about my friends and that writing isn't exactly your favorite activity," Elizabeth said, smiling slyly.

"Sheesh, I thought I was so convincing," Jessica said sulkily.

"I guess you forgot that I know you better than anyone else on the planet," Elizabeth said.

"I can't believe it—all that dull newspaper stuff and you didn't even believe me." Jessica rolled over onto her stomach. "I guess I was just so afraid of losing you as a sister and best friend that I felt desperate. The fact that I spent so much time with your boring friends should prove just *how* desperate."

Elizabeth rolled her eyes. "They're not *that* boring."

"Trust me, Elizabeth, they're not exactly the coolest

bunch of people," Jessica teased. "I'd take the Unicorns any day."

"Well, speaking of cool people, I have something to confess, too," Elizabeth said. "I had a lousy time at that party last Friday—or have you already figured that out?"

"I have to say, what happened with the Spin the Bottle game was a pretty big hint that you didn't have the greatest time," Jessica admitted. "I just wish you could have told me the truth about it."

"Well, I didn't want you to know that I hadn't fit in," Elizabeth told her. "After all, you made such a big deal about how I wasn't seventh-grade material, I wanted to prove you were wrong."

"I guess I was just the teensiest little bit jealous that you got to go to that party and not me," Jessica confessed. "I'm sure you'd fit in anywhere—as long as you're not trying to be someone you're not."

Elizabeth smiled. "Well, I'm *through* pretending to be someone else. And the only place I *want* to fit in is here—in sixth grade!"

"Hey, Aaron, wait up!" Jessica called to Aaron Dallas, her sort-of boyfriend, in the hallway on Monday morning.

"What's up, Jess?" Aaron asked, turning around and waiting for Jessica to catch up with him. "I haven't seen too much of you lately."

"I guess I've been pretty busy saving my sister from Spin the Bottle games and that sort of thing," Jessica joked as they started down the hall toward their first-period class.

"Speaking of games, I hear we're having a really cool guest teacher in social studies. He's a friend of my grandfather's, and he's going to teach us this game," Aaron told her.

Jessica frowned. "A game in social studies class? That's pretty weird. What kind of game?"

Aaron shrugged. "I don't know, but we'll find out soon enough."

Jessica giggled. "I wonder if it'll be anything like Spin the Bottle."

What kind of game will the twins and friends learn in social studies class? Find out in **Sweet Valley Twins 86, It Can't Happen Here.**

We hope you enjoyed reading this book. If you would like to receive further information about available titles in the Bantam series, just write to the following address, with your name and address:

Kim Prior
Bantam Books
61–63 Uxbridge Road
Ealing
London W5 5SA

If you live in Australia or New Zealand and would like more information about the series, please write to:

Sally Porter
Transworld Publishers
(Australia) Pty Ltd
15–25 Helles Avenue
Moorebank
NSW 2170
AUSTRALIA

Kiri Martin
Transworld Publishers (NZ) Ltd
3 William Pickering Drive
Albany
Auckland
NEW ZEALAND

Hang out with the coolest kids around!

SWEET VALLEY TWINS™

THE UNICORN CLUB

Jessica and Elizabeth Wakefield are just two of the terrific members of The Unicorn Club you've met in *Sweet Valley Twins* books. Now get to know some of their friends even better!

A sensational new *Sweet Valley* series, coming soon from Bantam Books:

1. Save the Unicorns!
2. Maria's Movie Comeback
3. The Best Friend Game
4. Lila's Little Sister
5. Unicorns in Love
Super Edition: Unicorns at War